A BRIEF HISTORY OF THE FUTURE, THE THIRD MILLENNIUM AND HUMAN COLONIZATION OF THE SOLAR SYSTEM

The Terraforming of Mars and Venus

Charles Joynson

All shall be well
Julian of Norwich

2000

One-thousand years ago our solar system was a very different place.

People had stood on the surface of the Moon but all of them had been white males. Women had been into orbit, but no children had followed them. No human had reached Mars or the Asteroid Belt. No human had looked down on Venus's boiling clouds or Jupiter's raging storms.

Rovers had been sent to Mars and some had survived long enough to send back images of its frozen desert surface. Getting a probe from Earth to Pluto or Uranus took ten years and no probe had yet reached the Kuiper belt.

On Earth two disastrous World Wars were over, but smaller wars were constantly breaking out. Many nations had nuclear weapons and threatened each other into peaceful mutual hostility. Healthcare was good in the developed world and people commonly lived to be eighty-years-old, but in the developing world healthcare was still basic and people usually died before they reached fifty.

There was also during this period great anxiety about Earth's polluted atmosphere. Over the previous three-hundred years the industrial revolution and the technological development of humankind had burnt massive quantities of coal, oil, gas, peat and wood. This had increased the atmospheric concentration of carbon dioxide to levels not experienced in millions of years. Glaciers on Antarctica and Greenland were beginning to collapse and sea level rise was threatening to flood low lying cities. Many nations were working to reduce their carbon emissions, but they first had to replace fossil fuels which were still the easiest source of power.

Human development was accompanied by mass species extinction. Conservation groups were struggling to prevent this, but the growing human population was causing habitat destruction, poaching and mass species loss. However geneticists were beginning to sequence thousands of different forms of life, giving the planet's lifeforms a final chance.

2020

To this date mobile phones had been hand held devices which required manual data input and instruction. In 2020 geographic trigger points began to link mobile phone geolocations to home and office devices. So a car driver could pinpoint positions and directions on roads near her home and link these to turn on of her heating, message her husband or order food. Office workers could trigger their office security, pay for car parking or buy event or train tickets. Other devices such as telephones and computers were able to turn themselves on when a person approached and off again when the person left the room.

Before the introduction of computers in the 1950s, documentation and record keeping had been done with paper and pen. After this, records were compiled using computer forms which required much the same sorts of information. However by 2020 devices and equipment begin to do things automatically which had to be done manually previously. So voice recognition and the proximity of other mobile devices allowed information to be gathered without writing and records were completed automatically. Additionally some forms allowed machines to trigger actions so fridges reordered milk, cars requested a service, pipes called a plumber and printers bought ink.

Hosted security shadow drones were introduced as part of security systems, these were loosed from wall mounted bases when an alarm was triggered and followed and filmed whatever triggered the alarm. This meant they sometimes followed a criminal, sometimes an innocent person and sometimes an animal. The same sorts of technology monitored many other sorts of crisis and allowed emergency service to know what was happening before they arrived at the scene.

Robotic devices begin to be used in people's homes. The most useful and labour saving were a series of robotic caterpillar-legged vacuum cleaners which cleaned carpets, stairs and difficult to reach places as well. To save power they don't suck but instead comb dirt and dust out of carpets. Robot artificial intelligent devices also appear in shops where they take over product scanning from human services people and in rubbish disposal sites were they separated recyclable and non-recyclable items. Like these, most robotic devices were single function and could only do a few tasks unlike humans who can do thousands.

Advanced fabrics appear in shops which do more than simply keeping people warm and looking nice. Some change colour in different lights, temperatures and humidities. Others change their insulating properties so they were warm in the winter and cool in the summer, and others generate power for phones and other devices.

2025
Hole in the wall artificial intelligence machines appear which help people deal with their banks, healthcare providers and other large organisations. They use voice, facial, knowledge, retinal, fingerprint, blood and pulse authentication and were far faster and less corruptible than websites. They initiate the process which sees biometric and knowledge based information becoming the key forms of identification and the cards people once carried disappear.

Websites using random biometric and knowledge authentication appear later the same year. They use the user's speakers to request personal information and check the evidence from the camera and microphone. However they are not as secure as the wall mounted machines.

Identification; whether in person or on the internet used the biometric rule of three. This meant that a person could only pass a security test when she had been authenticated by three or more methods. That meant that if a retinal scan, a finger print match and a knowledge confirmation all succeeded, the person was allowed access to information or resources.

2030

Survey satellites were sent to Mars to look for useful minerals, metals and water. They fired lasers at the surface to find out more about resources present on the red planet, and used radar to work out the depths of craters, lava tubes and sand-dunes. Lava tubes were considered to be good places to set up a Martian colony, but making them airtight was problematic.

Form filling, still a serious problem for many people from teachers to police was superseded by 2030 by activity detection using a new generation of artificial intelligence devices. These monitored activity using cameras, motion and proximity detectors and created records of activity which supplemented the information gathered through voice recognition.

Some schools and universities experimented with artificial intelligent examiners. These booths used voice recognition to ask the student questions and understand the answers. They were more accurate than paper or computer based exams and could vary the questions to suit the student's knowledge, speed and understanding.

2037

In the 2010s experiments had been made with augmented reality glasses. However the project failed because the processing power was too low, connection speeds were too slow and an adequate control system had yet to be developed. In 2037 the focus controlled swirling disk was developed which allowed wearers to focus on something and to trigger additional resources by selecting from the options Identify, Clarify, Qualify, Simplify, Magnify and Verify, all by focus alone.

The new AR glasses meant people could give up phones, pads, computers and televisions as the glasses could replace them all. The big advantages for users was that they knew more about how to find hidden resources, could use speech recognition and would never need a keyboard or keypad again.

The glasses also allowed real-time translation as subtitles appeared when people spoke languages the wearer didn't understand. This meant that wearers could travel to foreign countries without fearing that they wouldn't understand the language.

Other companies specialised in creating augmented devices for the other four senses; hearing, taste, smell and touch.

2039
Developments in artificial intelligence and the use of the AR glasses led to computer games being replaced by 'open-space' computer games. These were very popular with children and young adults and led to them deserting their bedrooms and spending more time outdoors.

The technology allowed users to use a stick, which the police preferred, to shoot at computer generated assailants within the real landscape. This led to many young people crawling and running through parks and streets, and pointing sticks at invisible objects. This was disconcerting to the older generation, but very good for children and teenagers. Young people hadn't had so much exercise since the dawn of the personal computer age in the 1980s.

This exercise revolution left some less warlike children behind. Therefore a number of innovative companies produced a range of location and chase games where children had to catch or locate each other and find hidden resources, again within the real landscape. A touch with the hand or 'counting coup' earned the player points which encouraged her or him to continue playing and to get plenty of exercise.

Open-space computer games received a great deal of criticism at the time as some parks became no-go areas for non-players and their dogs. Additionally some young people were killed on roads and in falls. However the games were so popular that they were impossible to stop and they became safer as the years passed.

2040

By 2040 much of the developed world's power requirements had been converted from fossil fuels to a mixture of nuclear, geothermal, weather and tidal energy. The secrets of commercial fusion energy continued to elude researchers. Lead, Cadmium, Nickel and Lithium batteries were essential for many electrical devices, but were heavy, expensive and polluting. The developing world was still primarily reliant on fossil fuels; however there was a good deal of nation building from developing to developed with consequential changes in energy needs and solutions.

Since the first nuclear weapons had been detonated in the 1940s, radioactive waste had been accumulated all around the world. Some of this had been stored in mines, but these had a habit of leaking either due to rusting containers or to fluid movements within the rocks.

Injecting nuclear waste through thin parts of the crust oceanic crust under the Cocos Islands in the Indian Ocean became a reality after geologists found it was just three kilometres thick. The advantages were that injecting waste into the molten mantle incinerated plastics and metals and locked radioactivity away safely and permanently. The hole was drilled from a rig on the Cocos South Island using high temperature and pressure drill bits and pipes.

Radioactive material was sealed into steel cylinders at source, transported to the Cocos and then injected into the hole using high pressure pneumatic rams. These pushed the drill pipes out of the hole into the mantle and the cylinder gradually followed it. The containers were repeatedly checked for leakage and the whole site worked more like a gun than a drilling rig,

2046

Whilst DNA sequencing has become ever more common in Universities around the world, it had been restricted to academics by the size and cost of equipment. In 2046 three companies in the USA developed hand held sequencing devices. With increasing data transmission compression abilities, hand held devices could transmit complete DNA sequences back to data repositories from rain-forests and other wildernesses. Thereafter millions of biologists were able to provide a last defence against extinction by sequencing endangered life forms.

Hand held sequencing was hugely popular with biologists at the time. Conservationists used the technology to collect DNA information from endangered species in many parts of the world. Volunteers used it to sample life both in and around their homes, helping to fill gaps in the data.

We now recognise that having lots of DNA samples for a species is almost as important as having a single species sample. So having many samples gives us evidence of a life form's generic diversity, without which we would have to recreate diversity and risk creating an imitation of the species rather than the species itself.

There was a great deal of research into the DNA of extinct life forms at this time; however technology was not sufficiently advanced to allow reanimation. Today we are very grateful for this work, as we can and do resurrect extinct species in many parts of the solar system.

This DNA sequencing revolution was not noticed by the majority of the world's population. But we now recognise it as a crucial step as it allows us to take life with us as data rather than in its more fragile or dangerous living state. This means that we can print the life when and where we need it. So for example we can print plants to give us oxygen to breathe, we can print fungi to recycle our waste and we can print insects to eat.

2050

Half of all bacterial infections were by 2050 resistant to antibiotics. This meant that patients and governments had to pay large amounts to pharmaceutical companies for the development of new antibiotics. These new drugs had an effective window of less than five years before bacteria became resistant to them. Their development costs therefore made them too expensive for most people without insurance or private wealth. Researchers began developing methods of enhancing the body's own defences against infection rather than using outside agents.

In 2050 DNA identification took over from biometric identification. It worked by 'sniffing' a person and identifying them before they could buy a product or receive a service. They would then choose the bank account they wanted to pay with from a screen. No cards, numbers or biometric information were needed unless they were flagged as being undistinguishable identical twins.

The same technology was used by doctors to discover health problems in people as they entered surgeries. Once they got to the doctor's desk he knew a lot about what was wrong with them and how to fix it.

Stable DNA mini-sequences were also used to identify individual products which made counterfeiting less likely and prevented people being harmed or killed by fake medicines, chemicals or foods.

2054
As the planet's temperature rose, many temperate parts of the world became wetter, both due to sea level rise and to increases in rain and storm. As wet places got wetter, dry places got dryer and bitter disputes took place between nations which shared common rivers. The higher nation would dam the river and channel its water to their fields, and the lower would buy tanks and guns. So it was in 2054 that the Water Wars peaked with many nations embroiled in conflicts that should have been solved by negotiation.

The number of nations with nuclear weapons also peaked in the 2050s as many more countries developed their own. However the total number of weapons declined as the developed world negotiated multi-lateral reductions.

The increasing numbers of people with weight, alcohol, drug and nicotine habits led to the rise of a movement which encouraged and expected self-control and will power. Members took an annual blood and body check and could show off their membership credentials to friends, family, banks and employers.

2056

The world's developing nations felt that whilst they were making huge efforts to reduce their carbon dioxide emissions, countries in the developed world were doing little but talk. The developed world's riposte was that they had made all the changes they could and it was now up to the developing world. The impasse which resulted was finally broken by the developed nations agreeing to engage in massive tree planting schemes which would look away millions more tons of carbon.

Thereafter developed nations used air seeding of large tree species in latitudes which had previously been permafrosted. They took stretches of farmland out of food production and planted trees instead and designated kelp forests as marine nature reserves. As these initiates were being put into action, marine biologists discovered a large increase in the concentration of algae in many of the world's oceans.

The United Nations had created a Civilisation Scorecard which assessed the application of Human Rights in a country. Scores were awarded for fair trials, education, free democratic elections and freedom from discrimination. This Scorecard was used by banks, insurance companies and trading partners to assess the risk and creditworthiness of an individual country.

In 2056 freedom from cultural mutilation was added to Human Rights legislation, specifically to put an end to female genital mutilation and other cultural disfigurements and tortures. This also included many practices which limited the freedom of women and many minorities, including discriminatory clothing, cultural identification badges and head and face coverings.

2060
Electric cars were common in the developed world in 2050s, but they were expensive and their range was limited by the weight of the batteries. In 2060

researchers looked again at electric eels and were able to develop carbon sandwich batteries which not only held more charge than traditional batteries, but were far lighter and less polluting. Electric motors quickly replaced liquid fuels in the 2060s in both the developed and the developing worlds. World demand for lead and oil plummeted as carbon batteries become cheaper.

Quantum computers at last became common after decades of development. However they were based in superconducting Q Clouds and devices such as AR glasses simply connected and the Q Cloud did the processing. With the increased reliance on connectivity, floating hubs were seeded into the upper atmosphere where they passed signals from Q Clouds to AR glasses and back. Powered by sun, moon or star light they were only replenished when they malfunctioned or their floats failed.

Regenerative medicine became an important part of a doctor's toolkit in 2060 which meant that damaged tissue and lost limbs or organs could be regrown like a lizard's tail.

2061
Smell detection technology had long been researched by universities around the world in an

effort to improve on the sensitivity of mass spectrometers. Breakthroughs were made in 2061 which dramatically improved the sensitivity of electronic noses; this gave airports a new way of identifying passengers carrying drugs or explosives. This meant the security services could retire the sniffer dogs which could identify heroin and explosives, but couldn't tell their handlers what they had smelt.

Thereafter static electronic noses were able to monitor the movements of people, goods and animals. So the police were able to monitor the movement of criminals and terrorists, zoos could detect escapees and shops were able to identify products being shipped or purchased.

2065
In 2065 a number of technologies came together to begin putting an end to war and terrorism. These technologies included the electronic nose, micro drone development, artificial intelligence and infrared object detection. The combined micro drones or Buzz Bees were able to detect explosives, fly onto them, activate a painful high-pitched alarm to allow people to get away and then detonate a small charge. These devices were designed to destroy ammunition and explosives, but not to kill people. They were able to use power lines and

solar panels to recharge their batteries and later models were able to camouflage themselves while they were charging. The first generation of Buzz Bees were ten centimetres long and vulnerable to weapon fire in small numbers. But in large numbers nothing could stop them.

Within months hundreds of thousands of Buzz Bees had been released from missiles, aircraft, courier vans and balloons in and over war-torn regions of the globe. The resulting demilitarisation killed a few people and injured others, but the majority were combatants and the peace that ensued was lauded by local people as worth the risk. The additional benefit for local populations was that they were much less likely to kill innocent civilians than the armed drones which had been used previously.

There was then an arms race between the developers of Buzz Bees and the companies developing explosives and military drones. However the Buzz Bees eventually became sensitive to all explosives and could destroy objects on the ground and in flight.

Buzz Bees like technology was also used at this time to locate drugs, land mines, radioactivity, chemical and biological threats.

2069

New developments in materials and sensing technology led to the introduction of clothes which help blind and partially sighted people see with their skins using tiny electrical pulses. Subsequently the same technology gave sighted wearers many additional senses. Augmented clothes were used in numerous industries to sense direction, chemicals, gases, electrical charges, dusts, sounds, acceleration and temperature.

Consequent to these developments the sensing torque was launched to give similar abilities to people who were wearing non-augmented clothing. The cold weather torque used two torques; one under the wearer's clothing and the other on top.

Improvements in battery and drone technology led to the development of free-living drone Bots. Fly and Swim Bots which provided communication, mapping and environmental information, and Seq Bots sequenced life forms in difficult to reach places.

2070

Although electric automated cars were now far more common than liquid fuelled vehicles, traffic jams were still common as it only took one slow vehicle or poor street component to delay thousands of vehicles. Some cities removed traffic lights at road intersections allowing automatic cars to maintain speeds at junctions and inter-weave through crossing traffic; however a single human driver could cause major accidents and fatalities. Some cities banned human drivers and imposed large fines for ignorance or disobedience, but humans continued to flout the rules.

Therefore a number of airports and city centres invested in suspended electrically powered pods which allowed people to be moved rapidly past stationary traffic to popular destinations. Their branching network allowed national, regional and local governments to expand the network at will and earn a portion of each traveller's fare.

The network rapidly expanded to replace both rail and road as travellers deserted the older systems for pods. The network further expanded to include metro systems, tunnels and bridges. Pod stops appeared in many places including ten floors up in office blocks. This meant that commuters deserted the streets, which became safer for pedestrians, cyclists and open gamers.

Bioluminescent lichens; using DNA from squid, were grown on homes and businesses in this decade to provide street lighting when power failed or was switched off. Other engineered bacteria and algae provided power for devices which would otherwise been damaged by power loss.

In the 2070s the internet of computers changed from a World Wide Web of information to the R Net of relevant knowledge. This meant that people were fed information triggered by position, direction, occupation and requirement. All this information was delivered through AR glasses and voice activated AIs. Most websites disappeared and activation engines appeared to replace search engines.

2071
An international manned mission to Mars had begun and was en route to the red planet along with the hopes of millions. Millions of others would rather have had the money spent on solving the world's problems. More probes had been sent to explore the outer planets and their moons, and commercial and experimental satellites were common.

The Mars mission had been long delayed due to the cost and the complexities of developing new technologies such as self-repairing suits, self-assembly rovers and safe-descent technologies.

On this first ten-month manned space trip real-time communication with Earth was impossible. Therefore the Project C was initiated whereby anyone on Earth with a webcam and internet access could ask an astronaut, cosmonaut or taikonaut a question, leave words of encouragement or make useful suggestions. Insults or negative comments were screened out by AIs and the travellers spent much of their time each day answering questions with a camera bot following them as they spoke and worked. This stopped them becoming bored or depressed as although not real time, they were communicating with real people who were interested in them and what they were doing, and they were able to create visual answers which would be seen by millions.

On such a long space trip they had to exercise for hours each day to avoid bone and muscle loss, and all grew centimetres taller than their original Earth heights. It was believed that they would adjust to Mars' gravity by gaining muscle and bone and by returning to their original Earth heights. The crew had an internal wheel ten metres in diameter which rotated fast enough to give them the experience and benefits of artificial gravity. Using it meant entering, strapping down, enduring the acceleration, unstrapping and exercising when the speed was sufficient to simulate gravity. Video walls gave the user the impression that he was stationary rather than spinning hundreds of times a minute. Additionally the wheel was internal because it was far less likely to cause atmospheric loss than an external wheel which had been suggested by science fiction writers.

On this first Mars mission a space had been created in the water tank to protect the crew from a lethal coronal mass ejection. Fortunately they didn't have to use it as it would have been very uncomfortable and closing the water plug which was used to protect the entrance would have made it even worse. Later missions either filled the inner wheel with water, allowing the crew to use it as a shield, or had a water tank shaped like a dish which was used as a shield between the sun and the sleeping module. In each case they had to turn the vessel to face the sun during a mass ejection as this gave the crew the additional protection of the rest of the ship as well as the water shield.

Earth's global temperatures had risen by one degree and Greenland's glaciers were continuing to collapse. Sea level had risen by half a metre and many countries were building flood defences and floating homes. Although global population was continuing to rise, birth rates were declining and projections suggested the world's population would peak in 2100 at 11 billion.

2072

The ship used for the international Mars mission was made up of four parts; a mother unit and three shuttles. They each had names; the mother ship was called Mother and the shuttles Red, Blue and Green. The mother ship was made up of five modules and the shuttles were designed to glide down to the Martian surface using huge controllable parasails, but could not return.

An additional escape pod could carry three people back from the surface to Mother and could be refuelled with oxygen and hydrogen. These would have to be sourced from surface water ice and liquefied using solar power. Mother had sufficient fuel to get back to Earth's orbit in an emergency but was meant to be a communications ship rather than an escape unit.

The crew was selected from the best international candidates and was made up of ten stable compatible couples and included two gay couples. They were all expert scientists, engineers, doctors and technologists, and all had been trained to fly shuttles. One couple were to stay with Mother while the shuttles descended to the surface to set up the colony. They would follow a year later in the escape pod.

The decision to send childless couples had been recommended by psychologists who believed it would prevent breakdowns amongst the crew on a mission which was likely to take the rest of their lives. Some were recent partnerships, based on common interest and ambition rather than traditional love, but the psychologists had assessed them to be successful and compatible unions.

They glided to a landing in a shallow sand filled stepped crater on high ground in the Syrtis Major region of Mars in December 2072, using thrusters to slow their decent in the last few kilometres. Once on the ground the thrusters were re-fired to dig the shuttles a metre into the sandy surface, extendable legs were deployed and messages were sent to the other shuttles and to Mother.

The landing site had been chosen because of its warmer equatorial location, the presence water ice, high elevation to avoid floods in a distant future, fifteen-metre deep sand and rocks containing elements essential to life and construction. The fact that it was a crater meant that the sand was stable and not likely to flow as might have happened in an old watercourse.

The crew's first job was to suit up through the suit port which kept dust out and exit the air locks on the top of the shuttles. They then had to begin the construction of a laddered tube which would allow them to get to the surface as the shuttles settled deeper into the sand. The shuttles would soon be beneath the surface protecting them from cold, dust storms and radiation, and the tube would work like an access periscope. They had additionally landed well away from Olympus Mons in case major landslides were caused by impacts or rain in a distant Martian future.

The next task was to collect the released parasails and to deploy them in their secondary role as solar panels; which were laid flat on the Martian surface and weighed down with stones and wires were fed back to electrical connections in a conical tube through armoured cables. These cables were part of the solar panel's emergency retraction system which deployed when dust storms threatened. Then a motor at the narrow end of the conical tube twisted the wire and the solar sheet back into the tube which protected it from storm damage. The motor and tube were anchored by being buried under cairns of stones which allowed the solar to be redeployed once the storm was over. The main electrical connection was fed from the motor to the ladder tube and coiled to allow the shuttles to sink without cutting the power supply. Earth's scientists had considered reinforcing the edges of the sheets and allowing them to be blown into the air like kites, but this had not been done as it was thought likely to cause damage.

They spent the rest of the month setting up chemical production systems in the shuttles, looking for mineral rich rocks, drilling for water ice and watching the shuttles sink.

2073

In January they were able to find water ice and to pump liquid water to the shuttles and to split it into oxygen to breathe and hydrogen for fuel. They located rocks with sources of Feldspar, Pyroxene, Olivine, Hematite and Kaolin. These supplied sources of Calcium, Aluminium, Iron, Sodium and Magnesium. However they continued to search for Chlorapatite for Phosphorus, Illite for Potassium and Sulphite for Sulphur.

They were also able to set up a series of wind powered atmospheric Nitrogen collectors and rock grinders. The Nitrogen was needed to make the air in the shuttles less explosive and the rock powders were for the chemical production labs. They found that it was easy to get lost in the endless Martian desert, distance and perspective were difficult to gauge and they had to keep direction finding equipment with them at all times.

In February the geologists continued to hunt for rocks containing useful minerals, the chemists continued to extract useful elements, the technologists began to experiment with cements, insulants, nutrients and glues, the biologists started to grow bacteria, fungi and plants and the engineers prepared to become miners. Lava tubes were too big to use for an early stage colony and the sand tunnelling option had been developed as a way to protect crews from Mars' harsh environment.

In March the ladder tubes were extended and the shuttles re-fired their thrusters to dig them down to bedrock where they settled on their extended legs. The colonists had their first taste of real foods for over a year in March as edible plants were grown in manufactured soils in their subsurface greenhouses and yogurts became available. Anything left over was fed to locusts which were first eaten as a source of protein in May. Initially the greenhouses had been planned to be on the surface, but extremes of temperature and the intensity of solar radiation had made this untenable. Therefore the first greenhouses were in shuttles and powered by artificial lights. Later they were in tunnels, and no plants were grown on the surface for hundreds of years.

Tunnel digging was then begun through the twin triangular airlocks at the back of the shuttles. The airlocks were locked together by bolts and capped by a three-metre shield. This shield had a series of ninety holes which had been plugged while in transit. The plugs were removed and a high pressure carbon dioxide tube was fed into each hole. This forced sand through a ten-centimetre hole near the base into sacks which were carried back through the airlocks into the shuttles where the technologists used it to make cement. The triangular shape had been chosen as the strongest geometry for the tunnels which determined the shapes of the airlocks and the tunnelling shield. Being underground on Mars meant they don't have to carry habitations to the planet, saving money and fuel.

This cement was then injected into aluminium moulds they had brought from Earth. These made triangular tongue and grove panels which would line the tunnels as they advanced out from the shuttles. The first few panels were made in the shuttles, but thereafter it was done in the tunnels. The shield had two components, the tunnelling shield which was advanced using pneumatic jacks attached to a triangular frame. The frame helped the tunnellers put concrete panels in to the walls at the right angles and positions. Water was sprayed into the sand so it froze and supported the walls before a panel was positioned and excess sand was sprayed back to the surface using compressed carbon dioxide.

The panels; which would have been heavy on Earth but were light on Mars, were glued together and to the substrate using an adhesive of Martian dust and cement. Once a section of tunnel was complete, the walls and floors were sprayed with three layers of airtight insulating self-repairing foam cement. Once these had dried, which in Mars' low pressure atmosphere was very quick, the first half of the triangular airlock was pulled into the tunnel and fixed in place using inflatable high pressure pillows. The section between the two airlocks could then be filled with air and tested for leaks before the rear airlock was advanced toward to the first. Moisture in the air was harvested using dehumidifiers in the airlocks and reused in making cements. In 2077 the tunnels connected all the shuttles meaning that the colonists could get between them without suits or helmets.

When not working on their day jobs, the colonists were still able to answer questions from Earth and camera-Bot their replies. This continued to connect the two planets, keep the colonists sane and keeping Earth's population involved. In May a hot spring was discovered two kilometres from the home crater which provided more power for the embryonic colony. The colony's biologists put a great deal of effort into finding life in the springs, but were not successful. The biologists however said that if bacteria from Earth reached Mars' surface, they would outcompete the Martian bacteria.

2081

3D televisions appear which don't require polarised glasses. They work using 3D printing to create and remove interference patterns on the inside of the television's glass screen. The printed lines created the 3D effect and lasted for a tenth of a second before being evaporated by a vacuum. The gaseous evaporate was then recycled and reprinted.

The first versions were slow and single colour and were used as demonstration models, however the technology advanced rapidly and full colour fast versions soon appeared. It gave people an alternative to watching films through AR glasses. There was some resistance to 3D television from people who expected the world to happen through their AR glasses and were deeply unhappy that 3D wouldn't work with AR.

In the medical world AI doctors appeared that could do in minutes what human doctors did in hours. They used DNA sniffing and other tests and analyses before providing diagnostic probabilities for a human doctor to decide between them.

2085

Massive fish stock collapse caused by plastic and chemical pollution and by infections due to the loss of predators such as sharks, tuna and turtles resulted in fishing communities trying to find other sources of income. A lucky few began working in the tourism industry, but the majority found work in industries considerably different from their previous employment. Sea fish were hard to find, diseased and expensive.

For decades sterilised male mosquitos had been released in their millions to reduce mosquito populations. Although this was successful in reducing the incidence of malaria, it did not eradicate it. In 2086 mosquito DNA was altered to prevent them transmitting the parasite. The release of these genetically modified mosquitos dramatically reduced the incidence of the disease and cut the number of people dying. Additionally viruses were added to their intestines which destroyed parasites and cut mosquito borne infections even further. By 2100 mosquitos were being used to immunise people against diseases, which meant they were not all bad after all.

Using yeasts and bacteria to make pharmaceuticals had begun in the early 21st-century, as had experiments in culturing animal and plant cells. Early forms of broth grown vegetables and meats had been produced in very small quantities, but scaling up was not possible until new highly oxygenated mediums had been developed.

Thereafter commercial companies started growing high value meats for specialist markets. The texture was recognised as being tenderer than real meat and foods could be produced almost anywhere without the need for fields or greenhouses. Some organisations began growing food in tubing attached to their offices. Thereafter many types of broth foods became available, and were soon more common in shops than naturally grown foods.

2090

Advances in synthetic photosynthesis, specifically spitting carbon dioxide into carbon and oxygen led to a proposal to site a solar powered facility in one of the world's great deserts. The Libyan and Egyptian governments agreed to their empty quarters being used for two major sites with rental income to be paid to replace their lost oil revenues.

All the building materials had to be supplied by air as the sands were too soft for wheeled vehicles. The factories were built to float on the shifting sand and wind baffles were constructed between rafts to divert wind-blown sand away from or under the rafts.

The carbon capture facilities get praised by the developing world which still believed the tree planting schemes of the 2050s were public relations stunts. Other desert nations go looking for projects which could earn them a living, stimulated by the loss of their oil revenues.

2092

The second Mars mission was launched in 2092 to resupply the colony which had been set up in 2072. The mission included two new shuttles, two tunnelling machines and three more reusable escape capsules.

The colonists had been able to make most of the things they needed to survive, but as they learnt more about living on a hostile planet they had created a list of things they wished they had brought with them in the first place. Their list included soil micro-organisms and insects, earthworms, ants and termites, bees, more grasshoppers, minerals, vitamin supplements, pharmaceuticals, sophisticated 3D printing equipment and more solar panels. Thereafter resupply missions left Earth for Mars every 15 to 25 years, bringing with them equipment, life and people.

The things about Earth the original colonists missed the most included foods such as fresh fish, smells such as roses and sounds such as the ocean.

Mars' dust storms were continuing to damage equipment as the fine powder disabled moving parts. The doctor in the Mars colony noticed her colleagues were losing more bone than expected due to the planet's low gravity. They therefore had to start wearing weighted clothes and after 2100 to take tablets to counteract this bone loss.

They had drilled into the rocks in and around the hot spring which had been discovered in 2073 to try and find life. Although amino acids and methane were present, no living things were found. If they had found life it might have delayed Mars' terraforming by hundreds of years. However the biologists believed that the process had already started as each human carried an ecosystem of bacteria, viruses and fungi on and inside their bodies and these were bound to reach the surface whenever they took any object from a shuttle to the surface.

2093
The advancing power of Q Clouds and AR glasses made speech recognition far quicker and more accurate than ever before. This meant that the very last keyboards were recycled and speech became the standard way to communicate with computers. Throat microphones also become common and more sensitive, which meant they could detect and understand speech without it being audible to others.

Pods had now reached every portion of the planet from Alice to Zanzibar. Rivers and seas have been crossed by tunnels and bridges and the trunk route through Alaska into Siberia was completed with a wire bridge in 2093. Crossing long stretches of ocean, particularly in seismic or Earthquake zones was more complex. In some shallow seas the pods were channelled through watertight tubes, but elsewhere air travel was still the only option.

Manual labour had become an anachronism at this time as robotic machines had taken over the vast majority of manual labour and repetitive tasks.

This left increasing numbers of people free to concentrate their abilities on creating, analysing, discovering, designing and inventing.

2095
In 2095 Greenland lost the last of its glaciers and ice sheets. This compounded the three-metre sea level rise caused by the loss of nearly 40% of Antarctica's ice sheets. Many coastal cities had to be abandoned as coastal defences were flooded and floating neighbourhoods were built.

In seaside towns hotels and villas were flooded by the rising seas and powerful cyclones and hurricanes. In some areas repeated storm damage made whole regions uninhabitable. People gave up their flooded homes and headed toward inland cities which caused disputes and Buzz Bees had to be deployed to prevent wars breaking out in formerly peaceful regions. They were joined on their desperate journey by people from mountainous areas which had become too dry to farm. After the snows and glaciers had disappeared their rugged homes had become dryer as the climate had changed.

This came to be known as the First Great Walking as 500-million people took to the roads. Many people blamed all their troubles on the immigrants which the press dubbed 'Minority Malice' because the incomers were not the cause of the problems. The migrants brought with them skills, knowledge and new explosives immune to Buzz Bees. They also brought the first Wasp Bots which could catch and destroy Buzz Bees by detecting the small explosive charge they carried. However Buzz Bees were soon switched to using an electrical spark rather than an explosive to detonate explosive substances. Flooded island nations needed rescue and fleets of ships were brought in to move them to volunteer adoptee nations.

The panic that resulted from the Great Walking accelerated the increase in currency sharing. A number of super-currencies appeared as smaller nations gave up their older coins and notes and took to using another nation's.

A discussion took place between the southern European, Middle Eastern and North African countries about a proposal to dam the Mediterranean. The concept would have meant sea levels being kept steady in the Mediterranean at the expense of a small rise in the Atlantic. However the discussions ended when it was realised that the damming would eventually turn the Med into a hypersaline sea devoid of life.

2097

It had long been known that giving old sick people blood transfusions from compatible young healthy people was very effective at helping them recover from a wide range of illnesses. In 2097 a commercial infusion was launched with many of the same hormones and growth factors present in healthy young blood. Tablets followed in 2100 but most health services refused to pay for them as they said they were not strong enough to be therapeutically effective, but patients took them in their millions; if they could afford them.

On Mars everything was recycled and nothing was ever thrown away. However plastics were in short supply as objects and for 3D printing, therefore they took to carving Martian minerals into useful everyday objects.

AR glasses give wearers new abilities, such as being able to see in the dark, seeing through fog and cloud, and being able to see the ocean bed from the surface of the sea. AR contact lenses were soon available and by 2110 the lenses of people's eyes were being surgically replaced by AR synthetics. People who preferred bright summer sun to sad winter gloom could brighten their environment and add leaves and flowers to the trees in the depths of winter.

Others who liked snow could turn their summer landscape into a winter wonderland and sci-fi fans or open gamers could create alien landscapes in their city streets.

2105

The last rhinoceros in Africa was killed this year for its horn. Even research establishments were broken into by thieves in the hope of stealing a few grams of horn. Many universities had rhino DNA but refused to bring the animals back from extinction until horns had lost their value. Both black and white rhinos survived in the Australian outback as poachers were more likely to die of thirst than to find an animal to poach.

Thousands of extinctions took place during these centuries of maximum human population and peak technological development. Some species were saved by conservationists and zoos, but these were a small proportion of the life forms which disappeared. Everything possible was done to collect DNA from as many individual life forms as possible. However some governments, communities and institutions prevented sampling, which meant that unless guerrilla samplers or Seq Bots were active, some species were gone forever.

On Mars the colonists were able to begin printing their own foods using resources they had sourced from their local environment. The printers had been delivered from Earth where printed foods had been added to tube-grown varieties some years previously.

On the Moon, a permanent base was set up in lava tubes close to the South Pole. Here they had light for their solar power arrays and frozen ice to supply the base with water. Being underground protected them from the temperature extremes on the surface and the airtight tunnels meant that residents needed neither suits nor helmets.

As the original Martian colonists aged, they had to be looked after. There was no chance of sending them back to Earth as the six-month trip was too much for people in their seventies or eighties, Earth's gravity would have killed them and the cost was prohibitive anyway. Therefore old age homes had to be built for them in the expanding network of underground chambers. Some of the colonists were doctors and phycologists, but nurses were now needed as well.

One good thing about life on Mars was that low gravity meant there was less likelihood of arthritis in old age, so people were able to live longer productive lives than would have been possible on Earth.

2108

Although the world's population was approaching peak and threatening to decline at the beginning of the 22nd-century, more land than ever before was needed to feed people. This was partially due to losses of farm land to flooding, partially due to the collapse of fish stocks and partly due to more food being needed to feed people's improved diets. People whose country had advanced from the developing to the developed world wanted more food, more meat and more luxuries. This meant that there was even greater pressure to turn forests and wildernesses into farmland.

Companies which had been helping to resupply the Martian colony began investigating the Asteroid Belt. Initially this was done remotely using space telescopes and lasers, but in 2110 two sampling and survey probes left Earth orbit for asteroids targeted as being rich in valuable minerals.

In 2112 three asteroids and a mini-moon in Earth orbit were sampled by autonomous probes and their value calculated as being in the billions of dollars. There was then serious discussion about using lasers to move these asteroids into Earth orbit. The idea was to use the laser to melt a part of the asteroid and use the exhaust gases to propel it through space.

On Earth some countries had made it illegal for the press to criticise its leaders. This allowed corruption, bribery and many other crimes to be committed by corrupt leaders. 2110 was the year of the three world presidents, with each being dismissed in turn for bribery and corruption. In 2112 United Nations Human Rights legislation was updated to include the right to a free press which encouraged journalists to investigate corruption amongst powerful people.

2114
Most humans in the developed world had nanoscale machine parts inside their bodies to keep them healthy. Some monitored and corrected blood chemistry, others helped them see or hear and others produced hormones and enzymes. These micromachines were injected when disease was detected and left in place until they stopped functioning or were no longer needed. They were mostly removed using magnets to trap them in one place, and then sucked out with syringes.

Shuttles were by 2114 using heat shields which grew and self-repaired. This made return space trips far safer as the heat of re-entry didn't affect the shuttle's structure or harm the crew.

2114 saw thousands of ninth-generation Buzz Bees being supplied to many parts of the fragmenting Russian empire, with both Moscow and the newly independent states receiving enough to prevent conflict. Politically this was a very troubled period, however despite the many angry words being exchanged between unionists and separatists; no children died during the split.

As the Martian tunnel network expanded linking shuttles and facilities the colonists had more time for relaxation. The options they had included reading, carving, writing, replying to questions from Earth, storytelling, playing board games and talking about food. For exercise they had a gym, could play squash, badminton and a hand shuttlecock game called peteca.

2121

By 2121 very few oil wells were still active and most oil companies were doing other things. Those which continued pumping were selling the oil to plastic manufacturers, airlines, shipping companies and classic car owners.

Pods now were the preferred transport solution for people and goods. The few remaining cars and trucks had been converted to carbon batteries and shipping companies were now experimenting with sails and super-large batteries. This left the airlines with their need for ultralight oils, but increasingly these were being manufactured organically. Only plastic companies remained and they were looking for alternatives.

Therefore Universities and commercial companies started looking at carbon as a possible alternative to plastics. Chitin, the stuff makes up human fingernails, includes carbon, Hydrogen, Oxygen and Nitrogen in its structure was soon being produced as a plastic substitute in large quantities. It had been used in foods, pharmaceuticals and fabrics for over a century and only methods of synthesis needed to be developed.

Some chitin manufacturers sited their plants in the world's great deserts because they could utilise the mountains of carbon produced by the carbon capture facilities. They could also take advantage of the sun's energy to power their manufacturing. They were also able to pressure mould chitin which had the additional advantage of being biodegradable and non-polluting.

In 2121 the first of the original Mars colonists died. He was over ninety and died of a liver cancer which he had fought bravely for 13 months. He was a Christian and needed to be buried, but had the bad fortune to die during one of Mars' furious dust storms which prevented both exit and burial. However if the corpse had been kept in the tunnels the smell would have been beyond endurance. Therefore he was put into an airlock and the air sucked out to leave him in a preserving semi-vacuum.

Once the storm had ended, a small team of suited and helmeted colonists carried the corpse away from the colony and used an excavator to dig a shallow grave. After a short ceremony the grave was filled in and they returned to the colony.

There was then a debate about how the bodies of non-Christians would be disposed of, as with no oxygen in the atmosphere and a shortage of fuel of all kinds, cremation would be impossible. Eventually after furious argument the decision was made that with no micro-organisms in the soil, burial could not mean burial as described in the texts, but just a matter of cold storage allowing for cremation when the climate allowed it. Burial on the same day as death was more difficult however.

2125

The first asteroid was targeted for mining in 2125 by one of the competing companies which had started asteroid prospecting in 2110. The press were expecting gold, silver, platinum or other precious metals, but the main resource the miners were seeking was water ice. Using two probes and a manned space vehicle the first asteroid was lassoed and towed to stable a Lagrange point where it was left for later use. Chunks were then sold to organisations and nations with lunar bases or space stations.

Half of all the world's languages which had existed in 1800 were now lost. Efforts continued to resuscitate them with the aid of old film and audio recordings. However the trend continued for the world's population to speak fewer languages. This was despite the real-time translation done by AR glasses.

By 2125 few people owned real paper or ibooks. However they still liked to read and the most convenient way to do this is on their AR glasses. These were programmed to allow the wearer to read while the field of vision was unperturbed; as soon as movement was detected the virtual book disappeared.

After almost 200 years of research, nuclear fusion was finally developed in a form which could be used to power cities, homes and factories. The first reactors were housed in large buildings, but as research continued they became smaller and easier to house and maintain. These developments meant the gradual disappearance of wind, tidal and geothermal power sources.

On Mars the colonists mainly ate a form of printed food made from a number of synthesised gluten proteins and water. The colonists complained that it was tasteless and needed plants adding to it to make it palatable. The plants had to be grown under lights which made them energy expensive, so the colonists asked Earth for more advanced food printing technology.

2134
It was in 2134 that the birth and death rates equalised and the world's population started to decline from its 13.4-billion peak. The great fear of the previous one hundred and fifty years had been increasing population; from this point forward the fear was of population decline.

Fifteen percent of all life on Earth was extinct by 2134 with cascading ecosystem extinctions being the most problematic. In these cases the loss of a single species triggered the extinction of many others which depended upon the original life form for their existence. In this way the loss of a small unremarkable plant led to the loss of the mountain gorilla and the loss of a single form of plankton led to the loss of three species of great whale.

Fortunately researchers had been sequencing their DNA for a hundred years which meant that there was a chance they could be resurrected. However for successful resurrection thousands of unique samples had to have been collected, which was not always true. In these cases a resurrected species was similar to but not the same as the original life form, which meant that even if it looked similar, it did a slightly different job in its ecosystem.

Additionally some more advanced species depended on learnt behaviours as much as instinct. In these cases infant nurture had to be done either by similar species or by disguised robotics. In previous times humans had done the raising of vulnerable animal infants, but this habituated the animals to humans which was not normally a good idea as they never became truly wild.

The first in a series of satellites were put into orbit around Mars in 2134. This improved the ease of communication between the two planets. It also meant that films made on Earth could be watched on Mars, resulting in feelings of homesickness. The things people missed most about Earth included the colour green; rain on their faces, children's laughter, sports and wildlife. Therefore a number of colonists volunteered to make films about Mars, which when viewed on Earth encouraged more recruits to join the colonisation programme.

Countries with a single political party or the same party in power for decades were not considered to be truly democratic, so the party was forced to split in two to give voters a real choice between party A and party B This action of the United Nations was hotly debated at the time as there were riots and protests, but in the long term it was better for citizens.

2138

A huge project paid for jointly by the Saudi and Omani governments began building a six-hundred-kilometre ceramic and high temperature alloy magnetic levitation track from west to east across the Saudi and Omani deserts toward Muscat; the Omani capital.

En route the track had to cut through numerous ridges and hills before gradually ascending the Jebel Akhdar ridge and rising to a maximum height of

2000 metres. At its peak the track was very steep at 25% off vertical and then came to a sudden stop at the top of a concrete pyramid.

When a vehicle was loaded onto the western end of the Maglev Skylift track and given a hydraulic push to get it moving, it was accelerated to the extraordinary speed of 40,000 kilometres per hour until it left the track at its highest point and began to climb into Earth orbit. Skylift was in effect a very large gun which propelled vehicles into a ballistic orbit.

The heat generated was enough to melt steel, but the magnetic alloys were protected by thick ceramic pads. The sound generated was sufficient to kill a person within two kilometres of the track. Therefore people in this sparsely populated land lived at a minimum of 20 kilometres from Skylift and then only with soundproofing. Muscat was protected from the sonic booms by the Jebel Akhdar ridge, but they could still hear it at night.

Once the shuttle had been launched, the bogie on which it had rested was parachuted into the Gulf of Oman. It was then recovered, sailed down to Salalah, loaded onto a railway wagon and brought back to the Skylift starting point for repair and recycling.

With the big steps forward made in fusion energy, both Skylift and the carbon capture facilities were by this date powered by brand new fusion energy generators.

2140

In 2140 the Fix Pill was launched on an unsuspecting world. DNA editing had been used for over a hundred years to correct mistakes in people's generic code, either due to damage caused by old age, or by inherited conditions. Each of these genetic mistakes had previously been corrected using molecular tools licensed by the world health authorities.

The Fix Pill was a combination of several hundred of these approved gene-editing molecules. They were designed to replicate themselves until all the genetic mistakes had been corrected within a person's body, which meant that only one pill needed to be used each decade. The pill was held in the hand or placed on any naked skin until it dissolved, which normally took about five minutes. People who swallowed the Fix Pill despite the instructions had to buy another. Very rich people started using one a month with the intention of living forever. They lived longer, but not forever.

The same DNA editing technology was by 2140 being used to fight infection. This was because many bacteria and viruses had common genes not present in human DNA. Like the Fix Pill the treatment dissolved on the skin and killed most infections in a few hours.

2149
In 2149 a confederation of developed counties agreed to pay an Oxygen Tax to developing nations to encourage them to keep forests rather than felling them. The developing world saw this as a dramatic turnaround as the developed world had spent three-hundred years paying them to cut their forests because they wanted the timber or the post-felling products.

Further communication difficulties between Mars and Earth led to satellites being placed at Legrange points the between the two planets. Leg Sats soon became important and were distributed into over five-hundred stable gravitational Legrange spots around the solar system.

2157
In 2157 prisons begin to be replaced by personal learning challenges for all but the most dangerous criminals. Prisoners were able to earn their release

by walking long distances across challenging and dangerous terrain. Some were offered assistance from local villagers en route. Others were subjected to challenges which helped them learn about the world, themselves and others. In the developing world people liked these challenges as they could earn an income as monitors, feeders, encouragers, controllers or teachers. Prisoners were not allowed to undertake challenges in countries where they spoke the same language. This would have allowed prisoners to seek temptations the challenge was designed to convince them to avoid.

With nations now peaceful and working together for the betterment of civilisation, nuclear weapons had lost much of their defensive significance. In 2151 there had been an accident with an old device where radioactive material had been spread over a wide area. Over three-hundred square miles of country had had to be evacuated downwind of the incident.

An international meeting to discuss the aging nuclear arsenal agreed that the vast majority no longer served any useful function and should be safely deactivated. However many countries were nervous about giving up their defensive capability completely. This led to the signing of the One Accord; where each country agreed to keep just one device. The target date was set for January 1ˢᵗ 2165, which gave each country plenty of time to recycle its arsenal and to inspect the arsenals of other cosignatories.

2159

In the early 22ⁿᵈ-century, biologists had discovered a species of monkey living in a highly malarial region of central Africa; which never caught malaria. Researchers eventually discovered that the monkeys had an organism living in their bloodstreams which was killing the malarial parasite.

This organism evolved as fast as the parasite and was transmitted by the same mosquitos which transferred it. It was species specific, which meant that no other species was able to use the organism to become disease resistant.

Humans were able to start using a genetically modified form of the organism to protect themselves from insect-borne diseases by 2169 and this kick-started the Symbiont revolution. Scientists developed organisms to fight human diseases and the inoculation was done by the insects which meant no campaign and limited costs.

By 2159 humans commonly lived to 120 years if they received good healthcare.

2176

The difficulty of transporting solar panels into space to power probes and space stations caused many entrepreneurs to suggest solutions. The problem was that they were both heavy and fragile. This meant that they were costly to get into space and were easily damaged once they got there.

No really good solutions were found until 2176 when a Chinese university student built a solar panel modelled on the design of a growing fern. To do this she created a tiny robot which could change its shape from flat to triangular in response to a cascading radio signal. When fifty or more of these micro-robots worked together they could unfurl like a fern. These fern panels were improved to be able to furl up again and launched into space as room-sized spheres which could expand to cover hundreds of square metres. By 2190 these fern panels were able to repair themselves when damaged by micro meteorite strikes. Many commercial companies continued to research and develop new nano scale robotics.

2187

This was the year that saw all the world's nations adopting a single currency which was controlled by the people who used it rather than by governments. This ended currency trading and stabilised global trade. It was also the year in which all Earth's children had access to free education up to the age of 16 years.

On Mars the colonists had found a way to create their own clothes for the first time. They recycled pre-used plastics and carbons, and turned them into fibres. These they were able to weave into cloth and clothing.

2194

The research into Symbionts started by the work done on malaria spawned a new industry searching for and adapting animal symbionts. These were found in many species, and their function and possible usage in humans was subject to a great deal of research.

Blood symbionts only existed in live-born species as they needed to get from mother to offspring during live birth. So egg laying species did not possess them; however they did occur amongst some snakes which gave birth to live young. Mammals were the main group of animals in which symbionts were found.

Parasites like symbionts were adapted to live on and inside other species. They were also researched and adapted to keep humans healthy.

2200

By 2200 there was no longer any difference between the developed and the developing worlds. Advanced industrialisation had reached all corners of the globe and all nations had access to advanced technology. There were still scattered regions of poverty, but they were isolated and not country specific.

A second Skylift was opened in Saudi Arabia in 2200 which incorporated a closed loop bogie return. This meant that once a shuttle had left the bogie and was on its way into orbit, the bogie was magnetically decelerated and looped back underneath the original track to be returned to the start.

2224

The continued research into animal symbionts discovered a bat hosted species which doubled the life spans of the bats. Initial scepticism was overcome when the symbiont was tested and proven to have the same affect in short-living species such as mice and rats. They then underwent successful testing in in cats and in macaque monkeys. Their first double-blind test in humans showed that they delayed the onset of aging by keeping blood vessels open. The organisation which had made the discovery commercialised the symbiont in 2224 at a price only the rich could afford.

Wealthy people also helped defend the company's intellectual property by not sharing their expensive purchase with anyone else. Press and pubic began calling the symbiont the Forever Bug. Patent expiry in 2244 led to far more people getting the symbiont, but the cost was still more than most people could afford.

Bats, sharks and crocodiles had also been the sources of a number of types of mitochondria which had been used to make humans more resistant to disease and more exercise tolerant. However they had also shortened lifespans which had limited their popularity considerably.

2230

By 2230 the combined commercial might of African countries had outpaced the rest of the world. The Africans were making more products for other countries than any other. Their labour costs were lower; their working hours longer and their hunger for more business was obvious to all who knew them.

DNA based computers took over from the older quantum computers in 2230. Quantum machines had always relied on a hub and spoke arrangement whereby the central computer did most of the processing work and the local just a minority. Even though quantum computers were at this time very fast, they were limited by the spokes which could be broken. When this happened, people's AR lenses lost almost all their processing ability; leaving the person bereft of information and guidance.

2236
Since the 2040s the two thousand people living in the expanding Mars colony had been forbidden from having children. In 2235 they protested this restriction and began reversing the sterilisation. The first children were born in 2236 and had to get used to living underground in airtight chambers. They adapted quickly to the low gravity but there were initial challenges in finding resources such as milk and nappies. The roles of some colonists had to change as the need for midwives, carers and teachers arose, and new specialists had to be brought from Earth to cope with the unexpected baby boom.

On Earth hunger and famine no longer existed as all nations; encouraged by the United Government; provided free education and food for all their children. Children from poor, marginalised, discriminated or education resistant communities were hot-housed in specialist training establishments.

These allowed parental visits and even family moves to avoid homesickness and child loss trauma.

2243

By the 2240s planetary warming had made some hot and dry parts of the Earth impossible to live in. After formerly vegetated parts underwent desertification people began leaving in 2243. In reality the Second Great Walking was more about fresh water than it was about heat. This Second Walking was done more in pods than the First Great Walking one hundred and fifty years before. However the disruption for the rest of the world was even worse as a billion people were on the move.

Because of population decline there was actually competition to adopt these refugees. This meant that unlike the First Walking this crisis was solved amicably without disputes or wars between migrants and adoptees.

2267

Long trip times getting from Earth to Mars caused many researchers to investigate new ways to increase shuttle speeds. New types of space propulsion were being researched, but little progress had been made. However in 2267 the concept of the lunar accelerator was proposed. This used the same concept as the Skylifts but would be built on the Moon.

The lunar accelerator was created using 3D printing technology to make a magnetic levitation track across the surface of the Moon. Firstly a cementation surface was printed followed by a film of conductive metal, and finally solar panels were printed to one side of the track.

Building a perfectly flat track meant levelling the lunar surface by removing boulders and hills, and filling craters and holes. The track followed the solar plane and only one direction of launch was allowed in case of collisions.

The 50-kilometre track was finished in 2289 and the first shuttle launched after arrival from Earth in 2290. However shuttles could only be launched toward Mars when the Moon was in the right position and then only when Mars was close enough to Earth to make the journey as short as possible, which up until the accelerator was operational had been just once in every twenty-six months.

In practice the accelerator's launch window was once a month during each six months of closest approach when the accelerator was mono-directional

and later twice a month after 2314 when it was converted to allow bidirectional launches.

2293

By 2293 the world's population had dropped to eight
billion and leaders had begun to worry. Around the
globe bounties were offered to women for having
more than one child and these increased each year.
Paralleling the population decline humanities' total
inventiveness was also declining. It had been hoped
that as artificial intelligence became more powerful
it would fill the inventive gap, but this had not happened to the extent expected.

Many of the world's forests which had been clear-
ing for agriculture and wood in previous centuries
were re-growing in 2293. A few had been replanted
by local people, but the majority were regenerating
naturally. Great efforts were made by environmental-
ists to replenish these forests with the pre-clearance
life forms. Some still existed and could be reintro-
duced; but many others had to be recreated from
their DNA.

Many species, which the conservationists would
have liked to reintroduce, had become extinct before
the generic sequencing revolution had taken place.
In these cases scientists looked for related species,

but if these didn't exist, they looked for bones, feathers, skins, fur, tusks and other remains to reconstruct the DNA of the extinct life form. They were helped in this hugely complex jig-saw puzzle by AIs which could find matches in seconds which would have taken humans months.

2323

The Third Great Walking took place in 2323 as sea levels rose another two metres. Again the migrants were absorbed into host nations because of population declines in their workforces. Many more coastal cities and islands were lost to the waves and some endangered species had to be moved to new habitats.

As the world's population fell to seven-and-a-half billion, drastic action was agreed by the United Nations which licensed the first birthing centres. These were hospitals where foetuses could be incubated using artificial placentas. There was opposition to these, but if women preferred to have one or no children, something had to be done to maintain the world's population.

The children were looked after jointly by genetic or adoptive parents and teaching organisations which gave the parents the freedom to decide when they wanted the children with them and when they wanted them in school.

Despite this initiative some families took to bringing up virtual children which could be turned on and off at will to suit their lifestyle. Virtual children had advantages over living children in that they didn't eat, cry, defecate or break things.

2343

The need to give Mars an atmosphere and to collect metals from the Asteroid Belt meant that better ways of shifting large lumps around the solar system were needed. Lassos had been used since 2125 but at least two ships were needed to collect each object.

Ideas had been proposed as far back as the 20th-century about using lasers to melt portions of asteroids and focusing the gas to drive them through space. Therefore experimental laser tugs were sent to the Asteroid Belt to bring water ice back to the Moon. The only modification that was made to the three-hundred-year-old design was that a funnel was used to direct the outgoing gases. This meant that the lump could be directed more accurately to its destination without causing too much mass loss.

2343 was the year in which doctors found a way to reboot the body's control systems. This meant that allergies, injuries and imperfections could be fixed permanently.

2350

Developments in nano-scale engineering led to a new generation of nano-machines, which could not only replicate themselves but could collect and move metals as well. There was great concern about releasing them on Earth as an accidental spillage in a university laboratory resulted in the building's collapse. The area had to be sterilised by having every piece of concrete and steel poured into a blast furnace at over a thousand degrees Celsius.

There was a risk that these nano-machines could proliferate and become an unstoppable infestation. However their potential for asteroid mining was realised at once and missions were planned to plant them on their surfaces.

The great advantage for the miners was that they only needed to plant a few nanos on each asteroid for the mining process to begin. They would then replicate themselves and channel microscopic particles of metal to a collection point on the asteroid's surface.

The early versions produced a diffuse mound on the surface, but later generations of these nano-machines could create cubes of pure metal ready to be collected by shuttles. Nanos were soon being planted on Mars and Mercury, and commercial companies made huge fortunes.

2355
In this year work began on extending the lunar accelerator right around the Moon. The reason was that having a circumlunar accelerator meant that shuttles could be launched all day and all night rather than just twice a month. This was important not just because Mars tips were becoming ever more frequent, but because more missions were taking place to the Asteroid Belt and the outer planets.

DNA based computers by this date included not just the four natural nucleobases cytosine (C), guanine (G), adenine (A), and thymine (T), but twelve synthetic bases as well. The additional nucleobases gave these computers extraordinary speed, storage and processing power.

2370
As the Martian colony expanded more biologists and geologists were needed to search for evidence of life. The biologists drilled hundreds of metres into Mars'

regolith and the geologists roamed about the planet hunting for fossils. The biologists found no life forms and the geologists found no fossils. Expeditions to the North Pole and various parts of the basins also failed to find any signs of life. Chemists analysed subsurface gases searching for methane and other evidence of life. They found methane, but believed it to be produced by volcanic processes rather than by living organisms.

Discovering other forms of life on any planet or moon would have given us new biological tools to help us colonise the solar system and in time other solar systems. For this reason huge efforts were and continue to be made to find life forms which didn't originate on Earth.

2385

To keep surface water on Mars so that it could have lakes, rivers and oceans it first needed an atmosphere to prevent water boiling away. Therefore air was needed before water ice could be brought from the rings of Saturn or the Asteroid Belt.

The source of water ice was hotly debated at this time as the moons of Saturn and Jupiter were potential sources, as were Saturn's rings. Most scientists believed that removing moons from any planet could destabilise the others and might result in a moon getting loose into the solar system. Other people opposed the mining of Saturn's rings as it would have damaged the most beautiful structure in the solar system. However larger lumps of ice in the Asteroid and Kuiper belts were realistic sources.

In 2385 the first large chunk of carbon dioxide was brought from the Oort Cloud and fragmented onto Olympus Mons. Other mountainous chunk of Oxygen and Nitrogen followed at yearly intervals.

By 2385 the world's population had declined to four billion, causing great worries to the leaders and prompting even larger bounties to be paid to women who chose to have children. When this failed to induce population rise, birthing centres were expanded to produce millions of babies a day.

The children born into birthing factories lived as part of a community family of 12 run by a single adult. They were educated by AIs with which they developed individual relationships. This meant that children could develop their own interests in conjunction to a super-responsive AI. When the children were young the AI took the form of a small friendly robot which never slept, but as they reached the age of five the robot was replaced by a virtual avatar on AR lenses.

This form of education meant that the birthing centre children far out-competed children from conventional families in intelligence and educational attainment.

As populations declined, people moved to be near friends and relatives leaving districts, towns and cities to disappear back into jungles and forests. This meant streets which had been devoid of wildlife for hundreds of years were repopulated by species never before seen in an urban setting. So bears in basements, leopards in living rooms and tourists watching fascinated.

2387

There was still debate as to the optimum composition of the Martian atmosphere and the target equatorial temperature. Some wanted an arctic wilderness, others a tropical rainforest and others a temperate lake-land. The Martian Climate conference took place during the long summer and decided long-term temperature strategy, including the amounts of water, nitrogen, oxygen, carbon dioxide and other greenhouse gases which were needed.

The critical argument focused on the amount of carbon dioxide needed to warm the atmosphere and give it sufficient mass to prevent it being lost to space. Insufficient atmospheric pressure might have made it impossible to make a hot cup of coffee but too much carbon dioxide might mean the ocean would be too acidic to support life. The conference agreed to look at other greenhouse gases which would create sufficient atmospheric pressure without poisoning or acidifying the surface.

There was also debate about future wind speeds and whether this would keep the atmosphere sufficiently mixed to prevent gas stratification and about whether to add inert or noble gases to Mars' atmosphere and any benefits this might bring.

The conclusion was that target should be for temperate lake-lands, which would mean the amount of carbon dioxide needed in the atmosphere would be far in excess of what was present on Earth. The congress also believed that the atmosphere would be sufficiently mixed by the rotation of the planet to prevent any pooling of heavy gas and any ocean acidification would be very minor.

2395
By this year the world's forests and wildernesses had recovered to an extent not seen since the year 1000. Lost ecosystems had been restored with reprinted life which had been extinct for hundreds of years. Some

species extinct for thousands of years had been restored to their former habitats and the planet's temperature had fallen back to levels normal in 1800.

The search continued for missing DNA of species which were ecosystem critical. Thousands of extinct species were completely missing from the DNA record, including many from around glaciers and other cold environments. Scientists were trying very hard to recreate them, but sometimes this was impossible.

Some missing DNA sequences were filled by DNA mining of old bones, teeth and skins of long extinct animals. Many resurrected creatures were missing their Intestinal viruses, bacteria and fungi which had to be estimated either from related species or from other animals in the same ecosystem.

In Australia Thylacines roamed the outback, in Mauritius Dodos were familiar, quaggas and black and white rhinos were common in Africa, mammoths roamed the Russian and Canadian tundra, river dolphins were back in the Yangtze and giant sloths disturbed travellers in the Amazonian forests.

By 2395 all of the carbon capture facilities had been switched off, leaving thick carbon granule deposits across the world's deserts. The last plastic products were decaying rapidly with even the most expensive antique pieces beginning to crack. History revealed that plastic had been a major pollutant forming vast country-sized floating rafts in the centres of oceans and so it was hard to believe when a single undamaged plastic cup could sell for the equivalent of a person's annual wage.

2405

In 2405 the clockwise and counter-clockwise lunar accelerator extensions finally met in the middle to completely encircle the Moon. This meant that shuttles could be launched to any destination within the plane of the solar system at any time of the month. This proved to be of great use not just to the Martian colony, but to commercial companies mining the Asteroid Belt as well.

2410

As water ice and frozen gases were brought to Mars, the atmosphere changed and the planet warmed. So the possibility of introducing living things to the Martian surface began to be envisaged. However the very first step was to create soil, or plants couldn't be grown and animals couldn't be fed.

The only realistic approach to creating soil on Mars was to bring whole soil samples from Earth, as each cubic centimetre of soil could contain tens of thousands of different types of organism, from bacteria, to fungi, viruses, algae, nematodes and protozoa. Therefore frozen and dried soil samples were brought from various places on Earth including many volcanic islands and mine dumps where the conditions were similar to those on Mars.

The regolith of broken rock was studied to discover which regions had a low enough salt content to make them amenable to soil creation. Regolith samples were taken from thousands of sites and these were seeded with soil micro-organisms from Earth in the lab to see what would grow and where. When this was better understood, the successful experiments were used to seed the Martian regolith. Then regular testing was done to see where living soil was developing and to try and understand why.

By this date the tunnel network extended ten kilometres from home crater and included hundreds of kilometres of tunnels as well as thousands of chambers with many functions.

2413
During 2413 people were able to breathe outside on Mars for the first time. The colonists' relief was huge and the children had their first opportunity to play

on the surface, but didn't know what to do or how to play. They were presented with a weighted football by a recent colonist and had no idea what to do with it. Once they were shown what it was for, the first game lasted six hours.

As portions of Mars' regolith were gradually changing into soil, other organisms were needed to help speed the process. Sometimes this meant secondary or even tertiary seeding with Earth soils, however once the regolith became living soil, micro-organisms spread without human intervention. Earthworms, nematodes and springtails were added at successful soil sites and these were monitored to see how well each species prospered. Some of these migrated many kilometres below the surface to initiate soil creation at new sites.

Later that year the first plants were planted on successful soil sites. The species used were volcanic island and salt tolerant specialists which could survive the harsh conditions prevalent before more water was added to the surface. Cold climate and temperate plants species were used as the areas of living soil expanded. Some survived, others did not. The reasons were not always clear, but mycorrhizal fungi, which could provide plants with the nutrients they could not get for themselves were thought to be a key reason for success.

Another problem was that although Mars had similar seasons, day length and planetary tilt, the Martian year was nearly two Earth years long. This meant that all life forms had to be able to survive double length winters and summers. Not all species could do this, but those that could, prospered. There was still a problem with dust storms coating the plants, however as more water arrived on Mars and the great basins filled, dust storms became smaller and less frequent.

2421

As soils and vegetation colonised the regolith around the home crater, insects were needed to pollinate flowers and produce seeds. Therefore bees, hover flies and butterflies were wanted to help spread life across the surface of the planet. Live bees could not be transported from Earth, so bio-printing machines were sourced from Earth's universities along with scientists to use them.

These machines used 3D printing techniques to create a single cell and its nucleus. Then DNA re-sequencing machines created the life form's DNA, RNA, mitochondria and ribosomes. Once these had been added to the cell, a small electric shock was used to animate it. The cell was then cultured using an oxygenated gel. This technique was used to create the first queens and drones. Once mated the queen bee would then build a nest and create the next generation of pollinators. In this way many different insects could be created to pollinate flowers and to help condition the soil.

The process of deciding which life forms to add to Mars was formalised in life lists. Each part of the planet had its own list, each list had branches which allowed the biologists to choose which species to add and when.

The first diagnosis of Mars Madness; a form of dementia was made in 2421. Doctors eventually traced the cause to a toxic mineral found close to the colony. The colonists had been carving lumps of it into household objects and works of art. Thereafter the outcrop was fenced off, the objects thrown out and the colonists told to avoid them.

2422

2422 saw an acceleration in the delivery of Asteroid Belt ice objects to Mars' atmosphere and impact into the low lying northern hemisphere. Some were angled to come in tangentially to avoid destabilising

Mars' orbit but the smaller ones were impacted onto the North Pole. As a consequence it rained much of the time, producing seas of mud in areas which had previously been desert dry. This deluge began to desalinate the soil and wash salt into the northern basin. To stabilise the mud, the colonists planted grasses which did very well and spread rapidly. There was great demand at this time for umbrellas, waterproofs and rubber boots.

Children in the Martian colony had to go to school just like their counterparts on Earth. However their schooling was far more focused on science and engineering than it would have been on Earth. As adults they would have to design, build and repair which meant that technical skills were crucial.

2425
The first food plants were planted in Martian soil in this year. Modern cultivated forms did not survive well, but many of the wild and indigenous forms grew rapidly and were easy to propagate. Simple tomatoes, chilies, grapes and leaf crops were successful and very good to eat after years of lab grown plants. Other successful foods included wheats, maizes, peas and beans. Root crops however were still too toxic for the colonists to eat, but experiments were

taking place with washed soils in the ground and in tanks.

This was also the year in which a few colonists moved out of the colony and began living independently in their own printed mineral igloos. They were considered pioneers by the rest of the colony who were keen to see how they got on and whether they succeeded in becoming farmers or if they returned to the tunnels in misery. The outsiders had to wear hats and skin creams to protect them from ultraviolet light as the ozone layer was only partially formed.

This was also the year in which the first cremations took place on Mars. Not all those who had died had friends or family who were happy with burial and respectful cremation had been promised as soon as it was practicable. The colonists had to dig up the frozen corpses and then to cut sufficient vegetation to get the pyres to cremation temperatures. Prayers were read by close colleagues and the ceremonies were recoded and transmitted so their families on Earth could share the experience.

2436

As plant life spread out across Mars' surface, pollinating insects proliferated to the point that the children were frequently being stung. Therefore it was felt that the time was right to introduce competitive pressure and predation, so the genetic sequences of predatory insects and spiders was printed and grown. Centipedes, grasshoppers and flies were released to continue the explosion of life across Mars.

As with plants, some species did well and others badly. As time went by other species were printed to niches that the biologists thought needed filling. This process was reactive to species survival and did not follow the carefully prepared life lists, which caused much debate amongst the biologists. Temperate tree species from parts of Europe, Russia and North America were planted in 2436 to ensure there was enough wood for the colony and food for the ecosystem animals.

Physicists had been studying gravity for hundreds of years and had understood how it made matter and space behave. So it was that in 2436 a gravitonic particle field was produced artificially for the first time, leading to the development of the gravitonic space thruster. This allowed shuttles to be accelerated to and decelerated from speeds formerly unimaginable. It made a journey to Mars just two months and to Pluto less than a year. The development of the graviton thruster was followed by the closure of the lunar accelerator which was used for the last time in 2451.

2440

As the more huge lumps of ice from the Asteroid Belt arrived on Mars, the northern depression started to fill and create Mars' first ocean. At the same time rivers and lakes appeared and resuscitated water courses that had last flowed billions of years before. The colonists had to stay well away from the northern basin and from the Valles Marineris inland sea at this time due to frequent landslides and tsunamis.

By 2440 equatorial summer temperatures on Mars were similar to summer temperatures in Sweden on Earth and just like Sweden the winters were cold with thick snow. The poles were by that time warm enough for the carbon dioxide ice caps to melt, increasing both Mars' warming and the amount of carbon available for plant growth. Some land areas slumped as subsurface ice melted creating lakes in unexpected places.

Very few colonists remained in the original tunnels which had been gradually converted into hospitals and laboratories. Many colonists had taken to farming patches of land and growing a variety of food and utility crops. Others had congregated and were living in three villages where they had begun to construct factories to print many of the products they needed. One factory made bicycles which made getting about much easier than walking. A few colonists had taken to mineral and metal mining with nanos and transporting valuable resources back to the villages.

Even at this early date manufacturing was far more efficient on Mars than on Earth due to easier access to materials and lower gravity. Work was started on a sky lift in 2440 which had to be constructed rather than printed due to Mars' fierce dust storms.

It was also in 2440 that a court house and police station was opened. The vast majority of people on Mars were well educated, obeyed the law and worked hard, but people did occasionally misbehave. A declaration of human rights was also published and a number of religious buildings were constructed including not just ones like those on Earth but non-denominational worship spaces as well.

2445

In 2445 the colonists met to debate land ownership. Leaders on Earth were trying to divide Mars up based on each nation's contribution to the Mars project. However the colonists believed that land ownership should be based on each person's contribution and subject to their productivity. A rudimentary Martian currency was proposed in 2445 and adopted in 2449.

The political situation on Mars at this time was like the political situation in the newly independent USA over four-hundred years before and as the Americans saw the British, so the Martians saw Earth's authorities. This was also the year that Mars got a government, for the people by the people. The authorities on Earth were not at all happy with these developments.

The next step in introducing life to Mars was the adding of fungi, slime mounds and arthropods to break down the increasing amounts of dead wood and leaf litter. This provided the pioneers with fertiliser to increase plant fertility and so augmented the amount of food and other resources available to the colony. The pioneers tried many food plants and grew those which survived and were easy to propagate. One of their favourites was hazel as it was both easy to plant and the nuts made excellent eating.

2445 was also the year in which Mars born colonists were able to make return visits to Earth. They shared history, religion and culture with Earth and really wanted to make the trip at least once in their lives. They hoped to visit religious sites like Jerusalem and Mecca. They really wanted to visit sites where great breakthroughs had been made; like the Outer Banks where the Wright brothers first flew and Bletchley Park where the first computer was created. And they hoped to visit the places where their ancestors had lived, worked and died.

The gravitonic drive made their visits possible, but Earth's gravity was a problem for them and they had to wear motorised exoskeletons to avoid collapsing with exhaustion. After a two-month visit, many were returned to Mars both tired and ill. They returned with them antique books, paintings and souvenirs to remind them of their history and their links with Earth.

2450
As rivers and lakes filled with dirty water, the colonists needed to seed muds just as they had seeded soils. Therefore dried and frozen river and lake muds were brought from various locations on Earth and planted in the silt. Later the same year phytoplankton, algae and periphyton were printed and seeded, and in 2451 aquatic insects and nematodes were added as well.

In the same year a deposit of kaolin was discovered in an ancient watercourse. The pioneers were able to make some rudimentary pots, but needed a potter. She arrived in 2455 and set up a manufacturing facility making good quality plates, pots and many other objects.

By 2450 the colonists were living in a strange mixture of wooden and modern houses. With wood being freely available at this date, many buildings were made from timber, wattle and daub. Most colonists preferred the pioneer lifestyle and liked to pretend they were living in eighteenth-century Boston. People who wanted a house became property builders not buyers as land and building materials were cheap and the only problem was the delay waiting for a building machine to become available.

2452
In 2441 scientists working from Earth sent a satellite to monitor Mars' atmosphere and found it was being blown away by the solar wind faster than expected. Therefore a series of fusion powered magnetic field generators were planned to sit between Mars and the sun as a permanent solar shield. They arrived above Mars' atmosphere in 2452 and were manoeuvrered into position in 2453.

Longer term alternatives which were discussed included using uranium to reboot Mars' magnetic field and introducing a new moon into orbit about the planet. The first was considered likely to cause radioactive contamination and the second might have initiated massive Earthquakes. Neither was within mankind's capability at that time anyway.

Allergies had always been a minor problem and inconvenience to the colonists but as the years went by they got worse. This was particularly so in people born on Mars and led to research into the causes. Initial attention was focused on the colonist's gut flora, but once that had been corrected non-familiar minerals and salts came under scrutiny. However as time went by these were proved to be blameless and attention was focused on the colonist's immune systems.

It was eventually discovered that of all the bacteria which had been seeded to the Martian soil, there had been a shortage of archaea and it was these which helped keep the human immune systems healthy. When these were added to the soil around the colony, the allergy problems diminished.

2460
As the need for pots and plates increased, the potteries needed to find more clay. Up until this point the mining had been done by people with machines. The printing factories were then asked to design

and print a generation of mining robots. The first of these was put to work in 2460 and a transporter track built to carry the clay to the factory.

By this time the ozone layer in Mars' upper atmosphere had increased to the extent that hats and creams were no longer necessary. Some colonists persisted, but the majority accepted the safety advice and took to wearing straw hats and no cream.

As Mars' oceans continued to fill, so did the Helas and Argyre inland basins. Smaller lakes and basins without an exit to the northern ocean tended to accumulate salts and heavy metals. This meant that nothing could grow in them except extremophile algae and bacteria. These micro-organisms had their origins in East African salt lakes and so flamingos were introduced in 2463. Mars' Valles Marineris canyon; 4000 kilometres long and 7 kilometres deep also filled and formed connections with the northern ocean.

2467

Ever since the first asteroid had been mined in the 2350s nanos had been used to extract and accumulate metals and minerals as cubes for later transport. The colonists believed that if nanos could make cubes, they might be able to make other structures as well.

This had not been researched on Earth because of people's fear of nano contamination. This fear was not as great on Mars where the desire to find and extract resources was far greater than any anxiety about contamination.

So it was in 2467 a way to customise nanos was found. This meant that they could be programed to create new structures and objects. Once the structure was complete and raw materials exhausted, a decontamination procedure was performed and the structure could be used.

The insect population of Mars had grown to the extent that the small insectivorous birds were introduced for the first time. Squirrels and jays were then added to bury nuts and seeds which meant less work for human planters. This helped spread vegetation across fifteen percent of the planet's surface.

2476

Ever since 2436 when gravitons had been produced artificially for the first time, scientists had been trying to create anti-gravitons which they believed had to exist as the universe was expanding rather than contracting. In 2476 this was achieved and a rudimentary anti-gravitonic drive was created. This initiated a new industrial revolution.

Just as the first steam engine initiated the industrial revolution seven-hundred years before, the gravitonic revolution progressed in leaps and bounds. Progress was similar to the development of the steam engine and like the steam engine people were waiting for a James Watt to create a device with practical applications. The first commercial anti-gravitonic drive was developed at a university in Australia in 2485 and this kick-started a storm of research and development.

By 2476 equatorial temperatures on Mars had settled in the target -5 degrees winter to +25 degrees Celsius summer range. Ice had replaced frozen carbon dioxide at the poles and ice age fauna including musk oxen, bison, moose, yaks, mountain horses and wild cattle roamed the southern continent. Woolly rhinos, reengineered from frozen remains and rhino DNA were added in 2481. Their primary function was the spreading of tree seeds. Rain fell frequently in the spring and autumn, and snow in the winter. Summers were dry with occasional lightning brush fires.

The last of the sky lifts in the world's great deserts closed as space tech switched to anti-gravitonic drives. The desert nations of the world started looking for revenue streams to replace their sky lifts and carbon capture facilities and began to investigate selling the vast volumes of carbon granules which had accumulated in their dune systems.

2486

In 2486 the world's first living organic computer was created. It used far less power than previous generations of electronic and quantum computers. Like the DNA computers it needed just supplies of water, amino acids and warmth. These allowed it to stay healthy and to build new neurons.

The first generation of organic computers used the same four natural and twelve synthetic nucleobases as the older DNA based computers. However this number rose as new synthetic nucleobases were added approximately every fifteen years to a peak of 42 in 2950.

In 2490 an organic computer was connected to a set of AR lenses for the first time and began to learn what people did. This was the first step in training early OCs to understand what humans would like to know and do.

The next generation of anti-gravitonic drives were produced and fitted into shuttles in thousands of factories around the world. These factories were run as competing businesses which were creating new patents and paying royalties to the original patent holders. This put pressure on the virtual money supply and the banking system as the demand for credit grew to be greater than it had been for over two-hundred years.

For hundreds of years humans had relied on a self-regulating currency. The money supply crisis caused countries to discuss creating their own currencies, and for international authorities to envisage a completely new world currency. The crisis was solved by developing a dynamic reserve as a way for the virtual currency to adapt to shortages and surpluses.

The demand for metals trebled the amount of asteroid mining and as demand increased, so did the number of new shuttles being dispatched to help. Both miners and factories wanted more and larger shuttles because the demand for access to space was doubling every year. People began to speculate as to whether anyone would be left on Earth by the end of the century.

On Mars the colonists received their first farm animals as goats, sheep and rabbits were introduced. Meat was a luxury previously unknown in the colony apart from occasional tube grown varieties. Food plants including coffee, tea, sorghum, oats and sugar cane were grown, and all were recognised as being considerably better to eat than printed foods which lacked the tastiness of natural foods. The first root crops were deemed safe to eat in 2487 as some soils were by then washed clean of salts.

2497

By 2497 it was recognised that early generations of anti-gravitonic drives were underpowered and inefficient. So the competing businesses began to improve their designs and acquire each other when credit ran short. The banks became more cautious as businesses failed and wanted better security from firms which could close at any time.

However as the number of factories declined, the power and efficiency of the anti-gravitonic drives improved. Shuttles were returned to have new gravitonic and anti-gravitonic drives retrofitted, and as the drives grew more powerful shuttles could be made larger. As the drives became more efficient, their fusion power packs were simplified so they could get to the fringes of the solar system. As competition reduced prices, shuttles which had formerly had short distance routes were fitted with long distance gravitonic drives. The same shuttles had their weight carrying capacity increased so they could take more people and materials into higher orbits or further into space.

On both Earth and Mars printed foods became better tasting and cheaper. The factories which produced these grew to cover many square kilometres on Earth and hundreds of square metres on Mars. The reduction in the need for farmland left space for wilderness and wildlife on both planets.

On Mars the great northern ocean had cleared sufficiently to allow life to be seeded for the first time. Thousands of types of plankton and algae were printed and seeded, followed in 2500 by soft- and hard-bodied corals.

2507

As research into organic computers progressed they became larger and more powerful. OCs began to go easily beyond their teaching and provide information and control not asked for but gratefully received. Soon they were able to solve problems in ways which equalled human creative ability.

The first signs of consciousness were detected in 2505 and this was proved in 2507. Thereafter they became ever more capable and useful, but some people worried that they were getting too intelligent and should be turned off and destroyed.

By this time more than half of Mars' surface was clothed in plant life, and as vegetation spread so did animal life. Birds, small mammals and insects were everywhere and the colonies hummed with life.

By 2507 Mars was producing and shipping vast mineral wealth to Earth. In return Earth was sending back ships, people and resources. However even though inter-planetary trade was producing wealth for both Mars and Earth, Earth's leaders still wanted more control over land and minerals. They continued to believe that Earth should own a large piece of Mars and do with it what they wished.

There was opposition to this view on Earth from the USA delegation which remembered their history and hard won independence from England. Curiously they were supported in this view by the English, but together they were in the minority.

As the Martians had control over nano mining and because the danger of contagion restricted their use to Mars, Earth's leaders could not force Mars' hand. Discussions took place amongst Earth's leaders as to stealing some of the more advanced nanos from Mars and putting them to use on the Moon. However the Moon was too close to Earth and the danger of infestation too great to risk. They considered the moons of Saturn or Jupiter but eventually decided that the risk of interplanetary conflict and nano wars were too awful to contemplate and it was better to negotiate and cooperate.

2511
As the number of companies making shuttles declined, they began to specialise. So some made shuttles, others cargo, passenger or goods ships. With fewer companies becoming more specialised they were able to accelerate production. At its height there were five-hundred-million people working in the space vehicle industry.

2511 was the peak year for patent filing, with hundreds of thousands of patents being granted for drives and ships. Innovations were made in loading, air locks, nano proofing, nano mining, docking and many other peripheral but important functions.

Interplanetary nano smuggling became a problem as people wishing to become rich attempted to bring mining nanos back from Mars to mine precious metals on Earth. The dangers of contamination and melting buildings and towns warranted heavy penalties.

On Mars, nanos were developed for multiple uses in these years, including manufacturing, building, synthesis, communication and decontamination. Dynamic nanos were also developed to change their functions after receiving an external stimulus. So the more advanced forms of mining nanos could be converted to decontaminate an area infested with legacy mining nanos, structure nanos could change their shape when it rained and synthesising nanos could create different fabrics.

Mars received a major life addition in 2511 as thousands of new species were printed and grown to maturity. Many more birds and small mammals were added, as were amphibians, reptiles and gastropods. As these species augmented Mars' ecosystem biologists worked to understand their evolving relationships.

2521
One of the most valuable resources in the solar system was carbon. One place this was plentiful was in Earth's great deserts where the carbon capture factories had left a layer of carbon granules over a metre thick.

Therefore a new sort of antigrav cargo vessels called Slugs were designed to collect carbon and deliver it to collection points to be refined and transported. These Slugs were modified in 2530 to do the refining and remove sand before they reached the refineries. In 2538 Slugs were done away with altogether as the carbon cargo vessels were modified to hover a two-hundred-meters over the desert and suck up the carbon through collection tubes. Baffles stopped sand grains moving upward and instead channelled the sand out though their sides.

The space vehicle industry was becoming more efficient as humans were replaced by robotic and OC machines. This left millions of trained workers without jobs, but as employment in the shuttle industry declined the space industry took off.

An interplanetary trade agreement was signed between Earth and Mars. Mars would continue to supply Earth with minerals and metals in return for resources and people. Cargo ships were now returning to Mars full of carbon from the Earth's great deserts to aid the expansion of life on the desert planet. This augmented the carbon delivered as frozen carbon dioxide in previous centuries.

2523
In 2523 the organic computer spine was developed to form a link between humans and organic computers

(OCs). These required a single neuron from the human to be genetically changed into a stem cell to include OC DNA and the DNA for an organic low energy radio wave transmitter. The resulting stem cell was re-implanted in the person's brain where it grew new neurons to interface with the frontal cortex and to use radio waves to communicate with external OCs. Because of the time it took to grow and form connections, the implant had limited effects on adults. However safety procedures required that adults should live with spines for at least twenty years before any were implanted in children or babies.

Mammal and bird predators were added to Mars' ecosystem in this year. The mammals included foxes, coyotes and lynx, and the birds hawks, eagles and owls. Bats were also added in 2523 and moles in 2524.

When Earth asked Mars for help mining the moons of Jupiter and Saturn, Mars agreed in return for concession rights to half of them. Trade across the solar system escalated to new levels with ships constantly on route from one rock to another.

2534
By 2534 adults had lived with organic computer neural spines for twenty years without any major problems. Therefore spine stem cells were implanted

in a group of 50 children and babies. These young people were monitored on a daily basis by scientists and their teaching OCs.

The colonists on Mars turned their attention to the northern ocean. They dropped large amounts of carbon granules into the wet and dry basins. As the water cleared they added more plankton and algae, followed by sponges, echinoids, stromatolites and other invertebrates.

Developments in dynamic nanos led to them being incorporated into the casings of ships to protect the crew and cargo against micro-meteorite impacts. The nano layer was generally about ten centimetres thick and the nanos were engineered to plug any breaches in the hull or in the inner walls.

2543
Martian holidays on Earth had become very popular as Mars' population had grown to three million and transport links had improved. Motorised exoskeletons made getting about relatively easy, but sleeping and relaxing in hotels was very uncomfortable because of Earth's strong gravity. Therefore a number of low-gravity hotels were opened in popular locations to allow Martians to relax in comfort. These hotels used antigrav technology to make the force

of gravity the same in the hotel as on Mars. This encouraged more Martian visits and they didn't go home sick or tired.

However these low-g hotels also proved to be very popular with people living on Earth which meant that there was competition for beds. It was therefore decided by the owners that Martians would pay just a fifth of the prices Earth livers paid.

The Martians were shocked by shallowness of many people on Earth, by their laziness and by their addiction to thing they saw as irrelevancies such as fashion, dancing, gambling and shopping. Living on Mars was a pioneer lifestyle which meant work, work and more work.

Newly arrived people from Earth and holiday makers on Mars had to wear weighted clothing to help them avoid painful falls and bone loss. When the Mars colony had been founded, people had developed pills to help them maintain their bone density. Later people took to wearing weighted clothes, as they prevented drug side effects, kept people's weight down and kept their muscles strong. By the 2550s a symbiont had been developed which kept bone density high, but some colonists still preferred the heavy clothing.

2555

One of the problems facing children and adults with organic computer spines was that they were always hungry for knowledge, but that they found absorbing it in conventional ways slow and laborious. So OCs were grown with hard-coded knowledge which spine people could absorb through their radio signal link much faster than they could have learnt in any other way.

Spine children were so fixated on their partner OCs that they preferred them to real people. As they grew older they took more interest in other spine children, but by that age they had missed out on exercise and developing human relationships. Therefore the spine adults were informed about the problem and invented the concept of interlacing. This meant that partner OCs could throw their knowledge and personalities between devices. This meant that they could transfer themselves between connection hubs and robotic devices instantly or exist on both at the same time.

The children also found AR lenses were more of a hindrance than a help as the images and sensual experience of the spine was far richer than the lenses. Ex-bots then developed an exercise and relationship training schedule which got the children playing cooperative physical games.

As the children grew older, they were seen to have perceptive control over what they wanted to see, hear, learn and what they wanted to ignore. So although the children were still behaving as individuals, they could learn from each other and from OCs without need for language or speech.

2570
When parents saw the spine children and realised how quickly they learned, reacted and thought, they wanted spine implants for their own children. So by 2570 thousands of babies were having spines implanted before they were a-year-old. By 2600 the birthing factories were implanting them into the brains of millions of babies each year.

Spine adults were much in demand as designers, scientists, engineers and planners in the 2570s. On their own they were quick, but in groups they solved problems like lightning.

On Mars the whole planet was vegetated and life was flourishing. Decisions needed to be taken about large predators, but the colonists were worried about the safety of their children and animals. However as deer were damaging their crops and hunters were having little effect, they realised larger carnivores were needed. So pumas, bob cats and wolves were introduced in 2573 and raised by robotic mothers which taught them to hunt and to fear people.

2580

The original spine children were now 45 and were so quick, intelligent and knowledgeable that people thought they were almost another species. The spine people were frustrated by normal people's slowness and could sometimes be rude and impatient without meaning to be unpleasant. The greatest difficulty normals found with spine people was that you couldn't keep a secret from them. If it was interesting, they all knew it. They had the extraordinary ability of being able to share experiences which to an observer looked like telepathy. So one could take part in an activity and the others would share the excitement.

As forests were restored on Earth and with the climate once again under control, snow fell at the poles. Areas of Greenland and Antarctica which had been forested since 2100 turned white with repeated snow falls and glaciers started to slowly rebuild themselves.

On Mars the first signs of evolution were seen as a single species of moth split in two, one living in the north and the other in the south. Hereafter other new species appeared to exploit new niches.

2595

Ever since the first colonists had landed on Mars in 2072, people had looked at Venus and wondered if it could be made into a home for humans. The problems with Venus were huge, as it had a thick carbon dioxide atmosphere, the surface temperatures were over 400-degrees Celsius and it had wind speeds of over 300 kph. The only way to even begin to make Venus habitable was to remove the vast majority of its atmosphere. But that of course was impossible.

On Mars fish and crustaceans were introduced to the northern ocean. The plankton and algae had grown so well that the seas had begun to turn green. More species of coral and sponge were introduced to reduce the microflora, and plankton-eating fish were added to speed the process. The introduction of other fish including carnivorous sorts was planned for 2695.

2614

Sharks, cephalopods and other carnivorous fish were introduced to Mars' northern ocean in this year. They adapted quickly to the food rich environment. A conference was organised by the colonists to debate as to whether Mars' oceans were conducive to marine mammals and reptiles or not.

The issue was that Mars' low gravity caused the ocean to foam and spray far more than any ocean on Earth, which meant that marine mammals might drown in bad weather. They decided to wait and see if the foaming reduced in time and to make a decision if and when that happened.

Other introductions which were discussed at the 2614 conference were Mammoths and Aurochs to help spread seeds and increase the amount of organic matter in the soil. The delegates decided go ahead with Mammoths, but to make sure they were afraid of people to keep them away from habitations and to monitor them closely in case they caused problems. Re-engineered Aurochs were considered too dangerous for even a wild ice age Mars and that the wild cattle which had been introduced in the 2470s did a good enough job anyway.

2623

In 2623 a conference took place to discuss the potential of Venus as a home for humanity. The possibilities were obvious as Venus was 80% of Earth's size and therefore was an important target for terraforming.

However Venus had lots of problems which made life on the surface impossible. In addition to the super-heated and poisonous atmosphere, it had a day length of over 100 Earth days, rotated clockwise unlike all the other planets in the solar system, had no tilt which meant no seasons and it was subject to periodic resurfacing super-volcanic events.

The conference produced a list of things which would need to be done as part of a terraforming project. This list was sent to scientists and engineers around the solar system asking them to find potential solutions and publish their ideas so that they could learn from each other. A second conference was planned for 2633 which gave them ten years to develop their ideas.

2625

The spine people on Earth had become annoyed by the slowness of their OC partner AIs. They therefore designed a new sort of organic AI. This would serve as a multiple user hub AI which could share knowledge and skills across thousands of spine people. This allowed them to freely borrow each other's languages, skills and knowledge.

They also became the core group developing solutions to the Venus terraforming project. Their natural interest in topics such as physics, mathematics and engineering gave them a head start when it came to discovering solutions as they were able to share problems and solutions using the OC hub to channel their thoughts. They did publish their findings, but their thinking was often months ahead of the discussion taking place amongst non OC scientists. Their developmental speed became well known to the wider population who wanted their children to have a spine whatever the wider family or community thought.

2627

Five probes descended into the upper layers of Venus's atmosphere in 2627 to search for life in regions with Earth-like temperatures and pressures. Two of the probes searched for anything resembling a genetic code. The others searched for structure and processes which would indicate the existence of life. No life was found.

As life grew to cover much of Mars' land surface and the basins filled, wind speeds dropped due to surface friction. So in the Martian Cetacean conference held in 2627 it was decided to introduce a single dolphin species, but to modify it to have a raised breathing hole. Certainly there was plenty for them to eat but they would have to be monitored to see if they survived the ocean spray.

Some of the most valuable items on Mars were the carvings made by the first colonists. The most sought after of these were so toxic that they were encased in lead glass cubes as they had caused the Mars Madness outbreak in 2421.

2633

In 2633 the second Venus terraforming conference took place to review the suggestions which had been made since the original meeting. The bulk of the event focused on the atmosphere and how it might be terraformed.

A team of biologists suggested seeding the upper parts of the atmosphere with floating plants or stromatolites which would excrete oxygen into an internal float. These could then screen the planet from the heat of the sun and as they bred they should build a layer which would grow to consume the whole atmosphere.

The principle criticism of the Venus plant proposal was that it might take tens of thousands of years to work. Another criticism was that only the top few hundred metres of the plant layer would be exposed to the sun and any that fell below this layer would be incinerated by the planet's super-heated atmosphere.

The second proposal came from a team of physicists who suggested removing the majority of Venus's atmosphere using nuclear explosions. Whilst easier to do than the first proposal, the criticisms were that this would contaminate the atmosphere with radioactivity and that very large amounts of carbon dioxide drifting around the solar system might be bad news for Earth's and Mars' atmospheres.

The third idea came from a group of planetary scientists who suggested creating a series of hollow or spongy asteroids which could be skimmed through Venus's atmosphere collecting carbon dioxide as they went. The difficulties with this idea were that although it could be done with nanos, it would need thousands of asteroids to remove the whole atmosphere and that the viscosity and wind speeds could cause collisions with the surface and could destabilise the planet. Additional comments about the asteroid skimming plan were that the asteroids could collide with other planets and that they would leak carbon dioxide to other planetary atmospheres.

The forth idea was from chemists who suggested bombarding the planet with calcium minerals which would lock away the carbon as calcium carbonate or limestone. However there was a lot of doubt as to whether there was enough calcium in the solar system to do the job and that it might take a thousand years anyway.

The last idea came from the OC spine scientists who suggested creating a portal into another universe to remove Venus's atmosphere. They believed that they knew enough to be able to create such a thing and that it would take Venus's atmosphere to a point from which it could not return and any risk of polluting Earth's or Mars' atmospheres would be extremely low. The criticism of this proposal was that it was completely impossible and even if it did work it might swallow the whole planet rather than just its atmosphere.

However the spine scientists proposed building a demonstration one way verse-hole in the Kuiper belt to prove the theory. They said they would use it to remove a small object from the neighbourhood of a larger body. Thereby they could demonstrate their ability to control the verse hole and avoid any risk to the solar system.

The last part of the conference focused on Venus's long day length and its minimal rotational tilt. All the proposals involved using asteroid impacts to change these. The maths and feasibility of the proposals were far more conventional than the atmosphere removal plans.

2640

The verse-hole experiment took place in the Kuiper belt in 2640 where the spine team had positioned two ice bodies side by side. The smaller of the two was just two-hundred metres across and the larger five kilometres, so being able to suck the small one into another universe without losing the larger would be a great test of control.

Intersecting particle beams were fired from six ships five-thousand kilometres from the ice objects and control was maintained using frequency and power output. The beams were focused on a cube of catalyst material which was attached to the smaller of the two ice objects and the experiment took place on March 17th of that year and went as predicted.

The two-hundred metre object was removed from our universe and ended up in another. The hole was closed successfully and there were no signs of any disturbance to our universe's physics or chemistry. The larger body remained where it had been and the experiment was deemed a complete success.

2651

Over the following eleven years the calculations were evaluated time and time again. Each step in the extraction process was debated and modelled repeatedly until the vast majority of spine and non-spine scientists believed it was feasible.

Atmospheric extraction was planned for January 2651when Earth and Mars were on the far side of the solar system. Sixteen ships were to control the particle beams to ensure that at least three would have contact with the catalyst at any one instant. The beams were synchronised to intersect in the upper atmosphere and to pan toward the surface over the course of twelve hours as the planet moved.

At zero hour the catalyst was dropped into the upper atmosphere and seconds later the beams fired. Then a furious typhoon was seen to appear in Venus's upper atmosphere. As the verse-hole did its work, people on the ships saw the swirling cloud expand to cover the entire planet. The white clouds were gradually recoloured red, brown and then black as the extraction point approached the surface.

The rest of the solar system was monitored in case the verse-hole's outlet appeared in our own solar system. However all was well and after eleven hours the beams were switched off with just 2% of Venus's atmosphere remaining. Photosynthesis would convert this into organic carbon and atmospheric oxygen once life arrived on the planet.

After the removal of Venus's heavy atmosphere, isostatic readjustment caused a big increase in the amount of volcanism seen on the surface. Whilst not a problem in the long term; there was a concern that the planet would be too volcanic for life in the short.

2653

On Mars there was a need for better transport across the planet. As towns and villages peppered the surface of the once desert planet, there was a real requirement for a better way of getting around than hiring a rover or shuttle for a day.

In 2653 the first pods were delivered from Earth with engineers to install them. The support network was constructed by nanos, which fascinated the engineers and the network began to spread out across the planet. Because of Mars' low gravity each pod had to be weighted to keep them from swinging in the breeze but they worked just as well as on Earth.

On Earth spines were implanted in foetuses still in the womb or in placental incubators for the first time. The mental development of these infants was far faster than in any post-birth OC children.

2654

As Earth's population declined to three billion, another thirty million had made it to Mars and the outer colonies. There were colonies on the moons of Saturn and Jupiter, many small colonies in the Asteroid Belt, a large colony on Earth's Moon and free-floating colonies in the outer solar system.

On Earth women were offered large bonuses for having children naturally, and smaller but still attractive amounts for having children in a birthing centre. The government tried hard to convince them that is was their civic duty, but fewer and fewer children were being born naturally.

Shops on Mars seemed very strange to Earth-born eyes. They were built on a slope which allowed shoppers to slide-shop from the entrance past the display shelves to the pay scanner where all their purchases were scanned and their bank account debited. They used board baskets, so shops were laid out as a single wide isle from start to finish and the pay scanners worked without needing them to stop or delay.

2654 was the year large carnivores including bears and Siberian tigers were added to the ice age species living near the South Pole. Very few people lived in the far South as the temperature range from -5 degrees to -35 degrees centigrade was too cold for most Martians. Debate raged amongst biologists as to whether Mars' long winter would kill any hibernating bears. However experience showed that winter temperatures were sufficiently variable to allow the bears to wake and feed rather than sleeping for the full six months.

One of the most common Martian pastimes was sky gliding from land, water and snow. The planet's low gravity allowed gliders to get far higher than they could have on Earth and to maintain that height for far longer. Mars also got its first dogs and dog sleds became popular in the frozen south. Although inter-planetary sports were a good idea in theory, the different gravities on the two planets made this difficult. Earthers playing on Mars needed weighted suits to prevent them flying off and injuring themselves, and Martians playing on Earth needed exosuits; which Earthers considered cheating.

During Mars' long winter, mineral carving competitions became very popular with big prizes for the best. Prizes were based on the mineral being carved and on the subject matter and on creativity.

2680

The plan to increase the speed of Venus's rotation which had been developed in 2633 was initiated in 2680 with the first massive twin rocky asteroid strikes. The impacts were on opposite sides of the planet and of equal mass and speed so as to increase angular momentum without disturbing its 225-day orbit.

Repeated twin strikes took place at seventeen-day intervals, which was the time needed for any wobbles to settle down sufficiently to avoid targeting problems. All together 48 asteroids impacted the planet over a period of just under 13 Earth months or two Venus orbits and accelerated the planet's clockwise rotation.

The asteroids and Kuiper belt objects contained many elements critical for life included iron, copper, manganese, zinc, chromium, selenium, lithium, cobalt, silicon, boron, calcium and a wide variety of trace elements. All of these had been chosen as they would be important for life in Venus's future. The planet's rotation was then allowed to settle for twenty years prior to tilt correction.

2681

As expected the 2680 the intense bombardment initiated a volcanic winter which obscured Venus's surface in thick swirling black dust. Scientists watching the planet waited only for the planet's rotation to settle as close as possible to 24 hours before deciding when to correct the tilt.

There was a worry that the impacts would trigger a volcanic resurfacing event, but although radar and infrared heat observations found plenty of volcanism, there was no sign of geological plates sinking. The tilt correcting impacts were actually more risky than the rotational enhancers as the danger of inducing a serious wobble was very large. However the sequence, masses, targets and speeds had been recalculated by OC scientists time and again and the formulae corrected as the planet's rotation settled down.

2692
In 2792 a conference on Earth's Moon took place to plan Venus's climate and temperature. Representatives from Mars were to lead the debate as they had more experience in the matter than anyone else. However Venus and Mars were very different as Venus was closer to the sun which meant it would be considerably warmer.

Much of the discussion focused on keeping the climate as cool as possible or it would be too hot to live near the equator. One of the suggestions proposed during the 2633 Venus conference had been to seed the upper parts of the atmosphere with floating plants which would excrete oxygen into an internal float. At the time this had not been taken seriously, but in retrospect it was considered to have value.

There was still 2% of the planet's carbon dioxide atmosphere left, which with the gases produced by the planet's volcanoes was fuel for photosynthesis to convert into organic carbon and atmospheric oxygen. However first the planet's tilt had to be corrected, the volcanic winter had to end and water, oxygen and nitrogen had to be brought to the planet.

2700

Each of the four twin impacts was planned to increase Venus's 3-degree tilt by another 5.5 degrees, with the target being 25 degrees; the same as Earth's. In May 2700 Venus's rotation settled as 23.6 hours, which was close enough to allow the tilt correction to take place. The first impacts happened at 01.23 GMT Earth time on the 27th May close to the north and south poles and the last on the 21st August. Then the teams waited to see what rotation and tilt had been achieved and if any corrections were necessary.

By 2700 Mars was 55% vegetated, 30% ocean and 15% ice, with forests as far south as the South Pole. It had seven major towns, extensive pod networks and many space ports. Mining was still hugely important as was nano research and development. People on Mars grew taller than on Earth and were only beaten by people from the moon and the outer colonies.

2714

Sea level falls and growing glaciers across Earth had led to many changes in coastlines and ice sheets. Since the last of the carbon capture facilities had been switched off, snow falling across Greenland, Alaska, Canada, Russia and Europe had accumulated ice to depths of over ten metres. Glaciers were moving again in valleys which had been ice-free for hundreds of years. Antarctica had kept 23% of the ice present in 1900 and there the snowfalls were heavier and ice deeper than in the Northern hemisphere. Across much of the southern continent another twenty metres of ice had accumulated as temperatures had fallen.

On the edges of Antarctica's returning ice sheets resurrected penguins were once again creating colonies. Leopard seals extinct for over three-hundred years were laying in ambush for unwary birds and fur seals.

Architects were working to rebuild some of the world's great lost cities. The jewel of these was Venice which had been flooded and destroyed despite attempts to dam its lagoon by rising sea levels in the twenty-second-century. The wave washed foundations of thousands of other coastal cities were being explored including Guangzhou, Calcutta, Mumbai, Miami, New York, Tokyo, Alexandria and The Hague with thoughts about their eventual resurrection.

2732

On Mars cities rose from the forests as the population increased. Homes, offices, hospitals, schools and pod networks were built by nanos as the planners catered for future colonists and children yet to be born. A city of the dead was created, modelled on Petra on Earth, with temples, mosques and churches standing sentinel over the graves and cremations of generations of colonists.

The tunnels the early Martins had dug so laboriously hundreds of years before had been converted into pod tubes which allowed travellers to reach city centres without being delayed by congestion. As Mars' nano revolution progressed, young Martians moved from their parents' homes in the country to universities, research establishments and testing facilities in the cities.

2754

Biologists on Mars had after over three-hundred years of terraforming and species introduction come to the conclusion that species introduction and the development of life lists was more like a highly complex game of Chess or Do against the planet than it was a simple list of species.

Like either game there were some strategies which worked and many which didn't, which meant that planning the introduction of life to a new planet was dynamic and evolving and that it was almost impossible to plan from beginning to end.

This was not just because some species survived and others didn't, but that evolution would change species to exploit niches they didn't fill on Earth.

2784

People had long wondered why humans had never received radio communications from other intelligent species. Scientists believed that the galaxy was full of them and questioned why we couldn't hear them talking to each other or to us. The Drake equation prophesied that there were ten-thousand planets with intelligent life in our galaxy alone, but for hundreds of years almost nothing had been heard. People began to speculate as to whether this Fermi Paradox was caused by advanced intelligences believing new civilizations to be dangerous and best avoided or if alien intelligences were exceedingly rare or if they didn't use radio waves to communicate.

Theories about past alien visitations had been discounted in the 2100s as there was only one form of DNA on Earth, which would have not been the case if the Earth had been host to alien visitors.

Then a team of physicists working on entanglement whereby subatomic particles in different places behaved as if they were the same particle discovered a class of objects which changed their states thousands of times a second for no apparent reason.

Failing to find an obvious cause, they started recording the changes and set an OC to analyse the sequence. After studying the problem for a week, the OC invited a growing band of 500-million physics-interested spine people to look at the problem. They analysed the problem communally for another week before saying that it looked like a code. The increasingly interesting problem was then published and cryptologists began trying to decode it.

2803

Over the course of a hundred years Venus's atmosphere cleared, the volcanic winter came to an end, the surface cooled and the planet's rotation and tilt stabilised themselves. The next step in the terraforming process was to create oceans and an atmosphere.

Thousands of frozen oxygen and nitrogen objects were brought by tugs-bots from the Asteroid and the Kuiper belts to be skimmed into the thin existing atmosphere. During the rotation and tilt correction process Venus's mass had been increased to 83% of Earth's which meant the atmospheres of the two planets were likely to be very similar.

Discussion took place as to whether Venus needed a moon, but opinion amongst mathematicians, astrophysics and planetary scientists was divided. Some thought a moon would stabilize Venus's wobble, but others said it had been stable before terraforming and so there was no reason it needed one now. This debate rages on.

2815

Venus's atmosphere grew slowly because finding large chunks of frozen oxygen and nitrogen in the Kuiper Belt was becoming increasingly difficult. However an atmosphere was critical to preventing the oceans from boiling away. The tilt and rotation were both now similar to Earth's and it was just a matter of time before the planet was primed for life.

Cryptologists working on the subatomic state changes found that although the vast majority of the binary code could not be interpreted, every 264 hours a 32-second segment was repeated. When this string was analysed, the first section contained 128 zeros and 128 ones. This confirmed that it was indeed a code rather than a random sequence. The second and third pieces of the code were prime numbers and the periodic table. The fourth section was three-dimensional shapes from cubes to dodecahedrons.

There were then three more sections in the repeated code, with each being separated by 64 zeros, and although the cryptologists thought these made up a key, they didn't decode it until 2858. There was lots of debate as to where the transmissions came from. However particle physicists said that it was certainly from within our universe and the source could be from any one of the billions of galaxies and any one of the billions of suns in each galaxy and from any one of the planets orbiting each sun. It is possible that we may find a location within the transmission, but they could be so distant from us that we might never actually locate the source.

2830

By 2830 there was sufficient atmospheric pressure on Venus's surface to allow the next phase of terraforming process to begin. This meant that more water ice was needed to create oceans, lakes, rivers and clouds. Lumps of life giving water were therefore brought from the Asteroid and Kuiper Belts to make Venus life ready.

These were skimmed into the top of the atmosphere in their thousands, creating a rainstorm which lasted ten years. Huge torrents tore down from the volcanic highlands into Venus's basins, ripping their way through mountains and across plains.

2848

By 2844 Venus had a complete atmosphere and large oceans. The pattern of the continents had changed as the impacts had added mountains of new land to the planet's surface. There was then more mountainous land around the equator than had been prior to correction.

Mid-summer temperatures at the equator were a sweltering 60-degrees Celsius and humidity was very high due to heavy daily thunderstorms. Cloud cover was thick and turbulent in the winter and clear and rainless for two months in the short summer.

Temperatures at the poles were much cooler at 25 degrees in the summer and 10 degrees in the winter.

Equatorial temperatures implied that people could one day live at these latitudes during the winter, but they would have to migrate as summer approached. Assessments were made about what sorts of life each section of the planet could support. Life lists and life game strategies like those developed on Mars were built to take account of Venus's challenging environment.

It was believed at this time and it is still accepted that each ecosystem on Earth provides a life list for a planet as yet undiscovered. So Earth's deep oceans provide life lists for ocean worlds, the deserts life lists for arid worlds and caves life lists for planets where all life exists underground.

Later that year ships above the atmosphere detected massive continued volcanism and large Earthquakes. Tsunamis were seen as a consequence of the Earthquakes and plans to land probes were delayed.

2858

Cryptologists had been working since 2784 to decode the remainder of the key to the subatomic code. These were a dictionary or thesaurus which defined thirty-five-thousand 'words' and their meanings. Each was separated by sixteen zeros and cryptologists are still working to decode these. Why the dictionary is broken into three sections is still unknown.

Now our physicists say they have found other subatomic particles which change state for no apparent reason. So there may be more than one of these alien broadcasts. One day we will know what they are saying to each other and perhaps even how to reply back to them.

Today we think that aliens already know we are here and know quite a lot about us, but are waiting for us to learn some key lessons. Perhaps it's how to decipher their transmissions and work out how to respond.

2871

By 2871 biologists were starting to plan ecosystems for planets targeted for terraforming and planets yet to be discovered. Each type was accompanied by a dynamic ecosystem game plan made up of thousands of species and their interrelationships. The planetary list included Ice; Hot; Desert; Deep Ocean; Shallow Ocean; Cave; Wind; Mountain; Savanna;

Volcano and Rain. Most planets would of course have a combination of environments just as Earth had all of them, but others may be of just one type.

2890

In 2890 the first multifunction probe was sent to another solar system. It was expected to take forty years to get there even with advanced gravitonic drives, which meant that it was too long for a human crew to even contemplate. However AIs were able to conduct thousands of experiments and analyses on route and send the results back to us.

By 2890 cryptologists had decoded some fourteen-thousand 'words' in the key to the alien transmission and were attempting to decipher the rest of the code. They had also made a start on four other transmissions and had found two new keys hidden in the new data. They believed that each of the codes was similar and they were either produced by the same civilization or by civilizations which followed the same transmission guidelines.

2894

Debates about possible sites for a colony on Venus led to probes being sent to various landmasses. The northern continent was the most likely target, but there were also new islands near the South Pole which were investigated. By 2894 it was obvious that some parts of the planet were still prone to regular large Earthquakes and massive volcanism and that the north was less active than the equator or the south.

Floating plants were seeded into the Venusian atmosphere in 2894. The modified plants fed oxygen into an internal bladder which made them float high up in the atmosphere. They had the effect of removing some of the carbon dioxide from the atmosphere and shading the surface from the sun's intensity. Any that died fell to the surface and added carbon to the regolith.

On Earth further increases in ice sheets and glaciers had led to a further drop of two metres in average sea level. New stretches of coastal real estate were being colonised again after five-hundred years of inundation. Cities long forgotten were rising again under old names and new, and a recreated floating Venice was again the jewel of the Adriatic and the world's top tourist destination.

2898

The Venusian life lists seeding strategy had been developed to the extent that the first steps in adding life to the planet's surface would be dynamic and determined by species survival. Scientists had then prepared ships with specialised functions. So the majority were able to print and seed life on the planet's surface, but others could measure the survival and success of introduced species and thus adapt the introduction strategy.

The first autonomous shuttles descended to Venus's surface in 2894 to begin the seeding process. As with Mars it was soil micro-organisms, nematodes and arthropods which were added on land and in the seas. The technology had progressed in the intervening five-hundred years to the extent that all life could be printed and no living samples needed to be brought from Earth.

Seeding timing was then determined by which species did well and so ecosystems were built incrementally. The high temperatures at the equator meant that the most heat-resistant species from Earth had to be genetically enhanced before seeding.

The ships which began the life seeding process were mostly small, as was the equipment which printed micro-organisms. Later stages in the life printing process created more advanced multicellular organisms and so needed larger printers and larger ships.

2919

It was noticed that life survived better on Venus than on Mars. Far more of the seeded species survived and prospered than had happened on Mars. This was put down to the higher temperatures and to the amount of carbon available for living things. There was also less salt in the Venusian soil than had been the case on Mars due to Mars' ancient oceans had extracted salts from the regolith and deposited it on the surface.

Life was seeded at deep ocean smoking vents on the ice moons Ganymede, Europa and Enceladus in 2919. These were driven by Jupiter's and Saturn's huge tidal forces and life could only survive close to their rocky cores as their upper oceans had temperatures as low as minus two-hundred-degrees Celsius.

2933

Like Mars, Venus has no magnetic field, so a magnetic solar shield against the solar wind was put in place in 2933. This protected the atmosphere and meant that it didn't need to be replenished on a regular basis. In the same year Mars' shield was replaced by a more powerful array. Mars now has a protective shield of 25-and Venus 49-fusion-powered magnetic field generators.

Discussions took place about reactivating Mars' core and natural magnetic field and whether Earth like plate tectonics could be started on Venus. The scientific opinion was that it was still far beyond human ability at this time and that if either was attempted it could do serious damage.

The thousands of cryptologists deciphering the alien transmissions had decoded twenty-seven-thousand words, and were beginning to understand some small parts of the rest of the transmission. However much of it was made up not of words but of some sort of machine code. It has been suggested that it may be a visual or auditory code, but as yet no one knows.

Thousands of machines were built to create a heat shield in Venus's upper atmosphere. These created reflective balloons with fabric repairing nanos on their surfaces. These were more effective than the floating life forms which had been seeded in 2894 as they were more resistant to sun damage and tears.

2950
The autonomous probe which had been dispatched to another solar system in 2890 finally returned data across four light-years of interstellar space in 2950. Its destination had been chosen because it contained

small rocky worlds in the habitable zone for life, as well as gas giants in its outer reaches.

The probe returned images and data of a planet which looked very much like Mars, with no evidence of life or of recent volcanic activity. Unlike Mars this planet, named Newton long before the probe had been dispatched, was slightly larger than Earth and orbited clockwise like Venus.

Scientists then began to search the probe's data for sources of some of the substances such as water ice, nitrogen and oxygen which would be needed for a terraforming project and a project plan was drawn up. This initiated by a series of Newton terraforming thought collectives and conferences in which the delegates discussed the sorts of things which had been done to make Mars habitable and to make Venus more Earth-like.

On Mars the concept of Dronic ecosystems was being developed, which meant that machines were able to design, manufacture, repair and recycle other machines. So long as a human was in control of the ecosystem the process worked very well in minimising the number of humans needed to organise large construction projects. Debate is still going on as to whether Dronic ecosystems should be seeded on planets which are not amenable to carbon based life. It is recognised however that in the life and machine combination is more adaptable than machine alone.

2965
Since the first asteroid strikes in 2680 Venus had been too earthquake-prone and volcanic to allow people to live on the surface. Men and women had walked on Venus as part of the surveying and seeding process, but it had been too dangerous for them to stay long.

Politics and land ownership had been debated hotly by authorities on Earth and Mars. Earth's leaders hoped to learn from the Martian experience and allocate land and power before colonisation. Mars, although less likely to supply colonists because of the heavier gravity, believed the Martian model should be followed with free land allocation and an independent democratic government.

However many nations and companies had paid to deliver asteroids to Venus. Some had been paid by others, but most had been promised a land reward and they wanted their geographic payment. The new land created by asteroid impacts had upset the allocations, but regular conferences had gone some way to resolving the issue.

The first colonists descended to the surface in 2965 when the quake risk was deemed acceptable and the double thickness ozone layer was sufficient to protect them from harmful ultraviolet radiation. Most of their habitation had already been created by manufacturing nanos and all they needed to do was to occupy and begin to run their experiments.

The site chosen for the colony was on the northern Ishtar Terra land mass, sixty kilometres south of Maxwell Montes, the highest mountain on Venus. Although this volcano had been extremely active between 2700 and 2850, it was by 2965 dormant with little sign of activity apart from the occasional quake.

The habitation was built on motor-sprung stilts which protected it from all but the most violent quake and the colony had been sited on a flat plane so that more modular units could be added as the colonists needed them.

They came mostly came from Earth and they found Venus's gravity very familiar. The few colonists who had arrived from Mars found the gravity as difficult as Earth's and had to wear exosuits in the early years to allow their muscles to adapt to their increased weight.

2970

By 2970 there were very few people left in the solar system without an organic computer spine growing in their skulls and advanced intelligence and communication abilities. There were a few recalcitrant old timers on Earth who wouldn't have spine neurons implanted in their children's brains, but they were few and considered very odd.

It had always been known that some of the water delivered to Venus would sink into its crust. This was already noticeable in 2970 requiring more water ice to be brought from the Asteroid Belt. As sources of water ice became more difficult to find in easily transportable very large lumps more had to be sourced from more distant parts of the Kuiper belt.

Moisture, moulds and rust were a problem on Venus which meant that any structure had to be resistant to water or it would deteriorate in the heavy daily downpours. Organic structures were far more resistant to these problems and the colonists began experimenting.

Cryptologists continued to work on the codes and had begun to make progress at understanding the meaning behind it. Much of it was about the nature of the universe, physics and chemistry. However other parts seemed to be codes within codes, but as yet we still don't understand those.

2976

On Venus the seeding machines were replaced by planting shuttles which hovered a metre above the surface and pushed plants into the soil using telescopic spikes. In this way thousands of plants could be planted each hour. The colonists had very little input into this process apart from watching it happen, as their primary roles were experimentation and analysis.

Tropical plants were introduced in equatorial regions affected by warm daily deluges and soon grew to rainforest proportions. These forests were too hot for people in summer and introduced life had to be tolerant of the sweltering seasonal temperatures.

Continued volcanism was adding more carbon dioxide to Venus's atmosphere, but photosynthesis rapidly converted this into organic matter and atmospheric oxygen. Debate continued as to whether the water sinking through the crust into the mantle would initiate plate tectonics. In Venus's geological past whole sections of its crust had sunk into the mantle in colossal resurfacing events. This had happened in the absence of water, so how these plates will behave in the future is unknown.

Analysis of the amount of carbon dioxide being produced volcanically led researchers to propose that changes be made to the life lists to allow for larger plants to absorb the excess carbon. As Venus was hot enough already it was definitely not required in the atmosphere, and no one wanted another super-heated planet.

2988

Once soil and plant life was growing successfully on Venus the first animal life was introduced. Using the life lists it was insects on land and invertebrates in the seas that came next. Soon the forests were humming with bees and shimmering with butterflies. The colonists ran their experiments and watched life proliferate.

Biologists were busy analysing the relationships between Venusian species and comparing them with those on Mars and Earth. In this way they hoped to improve the maths behind the dynamic life lists so that they might one day be used on other planets in other solar systems. New species were seen evolving from introduced life right from the very beginning.

As the organic computer spine became more advanced with new nucleobases and increased memory, intelligence and communication abilities, people found they spent more time accessing the experiences and knowledge of others and began to live as truly communal beings. Advanced spine people didn't need AR lenses implanted on their eyes as the visual experience of the world was delivered by the spine without the need for any optical aids.

This meant that there was less need for independent action and thought and more opportunity for communal thinking and decision making. Some people maintained a strong sense of individuality and refused to open their minds to just anyone, but the novelty of collective being was too much for most people who loved being members of a shared consciousness. There were many instances of people becoming so fascinated by other people's lives, thoughts, experiences and personalities that they failed to eat and starved themselves to death.

Others had similar though less suicidal problems, which meant they failed to keep themselves clean, forgot about their work commitments or ignored family members. As the years passed there was a gradual trend back toward individuality as people found they had no time for themselves and grew tired of sharing their minds outside of work.

We now recognise a medical condition called novelty neurosis which means that people are so fascinated by new experience that they lose interest in themselves and in the rest of the world. Examples from history include the first clocks and watches, the internet, cell phones, the first robotic aids and OC partners.

At this time although minority languages existed, everyone spoke Mandarin, Spanish or English. But spine people spoke the language of thought and believed that speaking an oral language was like learning to write Ancient Greek, irrelevant unless you are a historian. Some even began to give up spoken and written language and used thought instead which they said was faster and richer. They called this think-speech and said that no words or written message could equal the depth of a thought message with its sound, feel, smell, appearance and taste.

One new development which was made in these revolutionary days was the archiving of dead minds. This meant that if a person's spine was one of the more advanced modern generations they could save their entire knowledge and personality to a central

OC so that it could be accessed and experienced after their deaths.

2990

A mega-volcanic eruption on Venus in 2990 destroyed large tracts of forest. The colonists got away in shuttles without loss of life, but there was a great deal of damage to homes and factories. However the speed of regrowth was fast enough to give colonists the hope that the planet's life would survive such events. Despite such setbacks human populations continued growing on Mars and Venus and stabilised on Earth.

Insect life on Venus exploded as plant life proliferated across the planet's land surface. In the seas crustaceans and other invertebrates filled every niche and giant forests of kelp appeared around the land masses.

2994

As there was far more ocean on Venus than on Earth or Mars there was more rain and more rain-orest. With forests flourishing on Venus, humidity in the equatorial regions rose to the point that humans couldn't stand it for more than a few minutes in summer and the OCs controlling the life lists began to run out of high temperature species. Planting machines were adding new types of super-large plants at this time to soak up more carbon and biologists hoped that they could seed more high temperature tolerant species.

Mammals such as elephants, rhinos, antelope, buffalo, giraffe, great apes, cats and monkeys could approach and even cross the equator in winter, but summer was too hot for any terrestrial mammal. Extinctions occurred in some areas where seas blocked migration paths. Aquatic mammals such as hippos, dugongs, seals, otters, whales and dolphins were more resistant to the high summer temperatures but even they had to migrate to cooler climes in high summer. Large aquatic reptile species which could survive the summer temperatures included crocodiles, turtles, lizards and snakes. But without large reptilian herbivores other than giant tortoises the rainforests failed to produce enough animal protein to power the ecosystem as it should have done.

Birds did seem to be more resistant to the high temperatures, partially at least because they could migrate faster and further than any other animals. Ammonites, re-engineered from nautilus and squid DNA were added to Venus's warm oceans in this year.

The absence of large heat resistant herbivores forced biologists to look back through Earth's geological history to find species which could endure the high temperatures. They realised that it was Triassic, Jurassic and Cretaceous species which were needed, which meant re-engineering dinosaurs from bird, reptile, monotreme and fossil DNA. This will likely take hundreds of years as the best source for original dinosaur DNA are fossils which do not preserve DNA at all well.

Today Venus's equatorial regions are largely devoid of seed spreading mammalian life, so new species of reptiles and amphibians are being seeded by the automatic machines. Remote seeding of life will be a process we will use on planets in other solar systems, as autonomous seeders could plan, print and seed a planet long before any humans step onto its surface.

Personality sharing amongst people reached a peak in 2994 with billions of people sharing each other's characters. Today far fewer people do this as we prefer to know ourselves better than we know others. There is however lots of collectivism based on our interests and enthusiasms. People now share based on knowledge, experience, interest or thoughts.

3000

On Venus the safest way to get around was by anti-gravity plates which were stacked at plate stops and used nanos to quick grow safety barriers and rain covers. However some people took to sailing and hiking. Continuing Earthquakes and volcanism limited where people could live and work, but many were keen to test the bounds by living in quake-proof dwellings and having escape shuttles nearby.

Stilted towns and factories appeared across Venus as colonists set up their habitations and workplaces. Self-repairing nano materials were used to make quake recovery faster and more successful. As on Mars nanos were used to source materials, but more advanced generations meant that structures could be built by the same nanos which sourced the raw materials.

Life constantly surprised the biologists with its ability to colonise environments they thought too hostile to support living things. In comparison with Mars, Venus became a living planet far faster and with much greater diversity. Both planets were rich in the same sorts of igneous rocks, but the differing temperatures of the two planets were thought to be the reason behind the differing diversities.

3011

By 3011 an annual music competition was very popular with people on each of the three planets. However the different types of music led some to suggest the voting was more about planetary loyalty than it was about the music. On Venus theatres and Shakespeare performances were even more popular than music was on Earth or Mars.

3011 was also the year in which an OC biologist asked 'What's it like to be a whale?' and the first spine was implanted in one of Venus's marine mammals. The rule was that humans could follow but not lead, which meant they would experience what it was like to be another species, but they could not make it do anything as that might affect its chances of survival.

This sharing in the lives of other species has become hugely popular, the latest version of Novelty Neurosis and is called Extralifeing. Millions of people have taken to following a particular species or even individual animals and liked to imagine they had a relationship with the creature. Although the concept was invented on Venus, it has now spread to millions of people on both Mars and Earth.

3021

In the mid-2950s it had been realised that whilst Mars' principal manufacturing material had been its rich metal wealth, Venus's greatest resource was the carbon produced by its volcanoes. This would help life spread out across the planet, but could also be used to make structures and products.

It had also been realised that while Venus had too much carbon, Mars didn't have enough. Therefore hypersized cargo vessels or Hargoes were built to use synthetic photosynthesis to capture volcanically produced carbon from the atmosphere and transport it back to Mars as granules. The biggest of these can collect a cubic kilometre of graphitic carbon in a single load, helping to maintain Venus's fragile carbon balance.

Biologists then suggested that it would be a great deal easier to grow the things the colonists needed than to fabricate them. They then began to work toward this end by creating trees which doubled as homes with floors and rooms.

By 3021 many of these habitations were growing strongly and being lived in by thousands of Venusians. Some of these now look like enormous trees, mushrooms or mountains. Some have branches and leaves like normal trees, but others are covered in thousands of leaves but have no branches. Most use a mycorrhizal fungus to help them access water and nutrients, but others use bio-nanos to increase their growth rates.

The largest of these is a mountain like bio-city forty kilometres across and three-hundred meters high. Its rooms include sleeping chambers with grown ciliated-fibre beds to keep the air moving and fine water sprays to keep sleepers cool. The chambers have couches and tables all grown by the plants themselves and its eating rooms include fruit hanging from the ceilings, drinking water fonts in the walls, flowers to attract edible insects and gourds to trap palatable reptiles. There are even swimming rooms with waist-deep cold water, which on a hot day are a huge relief to residents and visitors.

These mega-plant habitations get something in exchange for all the things they provide to their residents; they absorb the carbon dioxide their citizens breathe out and they use their waste products as fertiliser. Planting bio-cities is simplicity itself as they can be grown from seed. Another advantage of these tree habitations is that they are considerably more earthquake-proof than built structures.

Bio-carbon engineering has even led to the development of living clothes which cool the wearer using their ciliated air-permeable fabrics which exude evaporating water films to suck away heat from the body. These clothes stay healthy provided they are immersed in water each night and worn in the light each day.

Other things which are grown on Venus include sun screens and shades, hats, shoes, and of course food. In some places sun shades have been grow to cover complete towns, transport plate stops and walkways. However anything mechanical or electrical still has to be built by nanos in the old way. Bio-nano trees were grown as living OC hubs which gave increased connectivity so that people didn't lose touch with the mind net.

3025

3025 was the year people began engineering their children for the environment. Like Mars the sparsity of human life made parents want to have more children. However in Venus's case parents actively wanted to make their children better able to cope with the extreme heat which debilitated most and killed some colonists. Some children had genes from Earth's rainforest tribes added to their DNA, and others went as far as to use genetic material from great apes and even reptiles. People now think that this could be done on all of the planets which we might colonise in the future and would mean humans diverging into multiple species.

This was also the year in which non-carbon life forms were planned for introduction to Saturn's moon Titan. This super-cooled moon was far too cold for any carbon based life form as the seas are made of hydrocarbons; the atmosphere is nitrogen and the rocks water ice. This work is ongoing and no life forms have yet been planted on the surface.

3028

A long running debate about Mars' magnetic field was resuscitated in 3028 when an interest thought collective was created to discuss the problem. The suggestions which have been made in the past involve the digging of a pit thirty kilometres deep and dropping radioactive materials into it. This pit would need to be about a kilometre wide and as near vertical as possible. The uranium and other radioactive minerals would have to be mined in the Asteroid Belt, cubed and encased in lead to protect people.

Each cube would be about ten metres square and would be transported to Mars using gravitonic power and lowered into the pits by anti-gravitonic drives.

Once several thousand of these cubes were in position in the pit, it could be filled in and the radioactive minerals should melt their way to the core and reactivate plate tectonics.

This will take generations to discuss and calculate. It may be that it will work on one planet and not another, and perhaps it will one day be a standard part of terraforming plans for other planets in other solar systems. But it would need to be done before colonists arrived on a planet.

Another subject which has been discussed was a huge solar umbrella to shade Venus and reduce global temperatures. Not only is this impossible at this time but it could be a very bad idea as well, as it might need the life lists to be restarted and could see many existing species become extinct. The general view is that Venus is a hot planet and will remain a hot planet.

The concept of creating a new planet out of the asteroids in the Asteroid Belt was also discussed in 3028, but considered too dangerous for any serious scientist to even contemplate.

3056
Plans are now afoot for to design ships to begin to terraform and colonise other solar systems. These

ships will serve as complete autonomous colonisation toolkits and be able to undertake all the key functions that terraforming will need. So they will be able to survey a solar system, locate a good planet for terraforming, source materials to make it ready for life and then begin seeding life on its surface from a DNA database of many millions of species. This will have to include the ability to create a complete machine (dronic) ecosystem and replicate new equipment using nanos and have complete autonomy.

However the key decision that has to be taken is; should humans be part of it? And if they are, could they cope with the complexity of the work and still have time to be human? And could we get them home after their posting had ended or would they be permanent residents in the new solar system like the early Mars colonists?

We now believe that our future lies in colonisation and that we will develop bands of colonisation like a series of spheres one inside the other around our solar system. So humans will be in the centre surrounded by spheres of; active life seeding; water ice and atmosphere addition; close survey and planet assessment and the outermost sphere distant planetary surveys.

If we can one day discover how the phase shift broadcasts are generated and produce them ourselves, we could have real-time contact with the terraforming toolkit and make decisions as a species no OC can make on its own.

3067

Cryptologists now understand the 32-second key to the subatomic transmission and have now begun to decode the rest of the broadcast. In time it will give us new technologies and new understanding of the universe. However there is a possibility that large sections are some sort of machine instructions rather than anything easily intelligible.

Today an Inter-solar journey is planned to a known Earth like planet using a verse hole as a transport channel. Our physicists believe they can aim a verse hole at a universe sharing the same physical laws as our own. They also think they can determine a verse hole's end point. Therefore they plan to send an autonomous machine into another universe and then for that machine to create its own route back to our universe. If this is successful the end point will be about 4 light-years from our solar system and will give us a way to cover the distance in just a few hours.

There was a time thousands of years ago when people travelled in hollowed-out logs, but then the human mind got to work and invented canoes, rafts, boats, ships driven by sail, wood, coal, oil and nuclear power. Then humans took to the air in gliders and developed internal combustion and then jet engines.

More recently our ancestors have done the same in space, developing liquid fuelled rockets, gravitonic and anti-gravitonic drives. Verse holes are likely to be the start of a new sort of technological inventive leap from simple holes to something else. Perhaps we will one day have verse hole transport networks.

We now regard our global ecosystem as an interconnected network of all the life on Earth and call this Planetary Ecosystem a Plec. Since then we have come to believe that our Plec is just one of many and that each of them has life and reproduction cycles.

When we look for evidence of our Plec reproducing, we can see that we have seeded life on Mars and Venus, and that this probably exemplifies the way life is reproduced by other Plecs. Therefore we assume that any intelligent species which has the ability to manipulate matter, communicate and be inventive forms the reproductive organ of its Plec. And this means that humanity is Earth's Plec flower.

This also leads us to think that Plec forests with common origins are interested in each other or in other forests, but not in isolated self-starting intelligences or 'sports' like us.

Charles Joynson is either:

A lost historian from the 31st century
Or
A futurist maven
Or
The pen name of a professor of astrophysics
Or
An anti-extinction conservationist
You choose.